Little Devil

BETHANY WINTERS

Copyright

Copyright © 2021 by Bethany Winters

All rights Reserved.

No part of this book may be reproduced or used in any manner without written permission of the copyright owner except for the use of quotations in a book review.

This is a work of fiction. Names, characters, places and incidents are either the product of the author's imagination or are used fictitiously. Any resemblance to actual persons, living or dead, events, or locales is entirely coincidental.

Photography, Cover Design & Formatting by TalkNerdy2Me
www.thetalknerdy.com

American Idiot – Green Day
Ferrari – Bebe Rexha
21st Century Vampire – Lil Huddy
Teardrops – Bring Me The Horizon
Rumors – Neffex
Bloody Valentine – Machine Gun Kelly
Never Be The Same – Camila Cabello
Cotton Candy – Yungblud
Slow Down – Chase Atlantic
This Feeling – The Chainsmokers & Kelsea Ballerini
Sugar, We're Goin' Down – Fall Out Boy
Sk8er Boi – Avril Lavigne
Immortals – Fall Out Boy

Little Devil

"No two people are the same. And *that* is the beauty about people. Different is amazing. Embrace those who aren't like you, for everyone has something to offer."

– K. Webster

To the bad boy I married.
Your driving still scares me.

Little Devil

1

Xander

"You're such a fucking loser, Xan!"

I wince at the sound of her insanely squeaky voice echoing through the otherwise silent house, quickly ducking for cover when she tosses her black stiletto across the entryway, aiming for my face.

Crazy ass bitch.

The smoking hot brunette whose name I've forgotten glares, bending over to snatch the other shoe from her foot. "What did you just call me?"

Fucking hell.

"Babe," I say softly, lifting my hands up in an attempt to diffuse the unfortunate situation I've found myself in. "I said I was sorr–"

"But you're *not*!" she screams, throwing her shoe at my chest. "You're fucking *laughing* at me right now, asshole. You're not sorry at all."

"I'm not laughing at you."

Her nostrils flare and I pinch my lips together, figuring it's safe to stalk towards her now that she's out of weapons. I met this girl at Justin's after party last night and it seems I've personally offended her by fucking her, accidentally allowing her to fall asleep in my bed at four in the morning, and then calling her the wrong name while asking her to leave just now.

To say she's furious would be putting it lightly, and it's taking everything I have not to burst out laughing.

Her eyes narrow like she knows it and I cringe, mentally bracing myself for what I know comes next. I open my mouth to offer some sort of peace offering before she starts screaming like a maniac, just like they always do, but then she shocks the shit out of me and sucker punches me in the face. I pull my head back and lift a hand up to my mouth, pulling it away to examine the blood coating my fingertips.

"Damn, girl," I mutter, oddly impressed by the balls on this chick. "That fucking *hurts*."

She grins, pleased with herself and the shock on my face, no doubt. With that, she snatches her heels from the floor and turns to leave, flipping me off over her shoulder while she swings the front door open.

"Nice meeting you, *Xander Reid*," she calls, sarcastic as shit. "Tell Justin I said thanks a lot for setting me up with Hollywood's biggest let down. I had a blast."

I crack a smile and move to follow her, honest to god wondering if she'll fuck me with all that spunk she's kept hidden until now, but then I spot the three motorcycles parked on my driveway and freeze where I stand. The biggest guy of the three – the one who just so happens to look a lot like the girl who just hit me – tosses her his helmet and climbs off of his bike, headed this way like he's ready to snap my neck.

"Oh, fuck."

"Come here, you little shit!"

I'm not *little*, but I'm not stupid, either, which is why I have no shame in running away from him to get back to the safety of my own house. I move to do just that, but I don't get the chance before he snatches the back of my neck and spins me to face him. Noting the fury in his eyes, I open my mouth to do what I do best, ready to talk myself out of this, but then I'm met with yet another fist to the face – a meaner one this time. He punches me in the nose and I hit the concrete, groaning at the pain shooting up my spine and through my probably cracked skull.

"Jesus, fuck, man," I hiss, lifting my hands to cover the sore spot. "What're you a family of boxers or some shit?"

Laughter rings out around me and I take that as a yes, squinting at the mid morning sun while I wait for them to leave. As soon as the sound of their engines fades into the distance, I let out a heavy sigh and force myself up to stand, half waving at the nosey next door neighbor slash eighty year old bitch who gets off on ratting me out to my parents.

"Mornin', Felicia."

Her wrinkled mouth forms a rare, sinister grin like she knows something I don't and she waves right back, making me shudder. I stumble through the front door and lock it behind me, quickly setting the alarm in case they decide to come back for more. My nose hurts like a motherfucker, but a quick look in the mirror tells me he didn't break it. I can already tell I'm about to be walking around with a nasty black eye to match the busted up lip his little sister gave me, though.

I remove my nose rings from both nostrils and run a hand through my hair, messing it up until it sticks out the way I like it. I keep the sides cut short but the top is long and dark, the ends dyed a deep shade of purple. My eyes drop to the silver cross sitting around my neck and I smile sadly at it, backing away from my own reflection to head for the kitchen. I wash my piercings at the sink and rinse them off with some saline solution, side eyeing my four year old Rottweiler while I grab a couple paper towels to dry them off.

"Some guard dog you are," I mutter, tilting my head at the front door. "They coulda killed me out there, man."

He scratches my thigh with his big ass paw and I laugh lightly, ruffling the short hair beneath his chin while I grab his food from the cabinet overhead. I used to keep it in the pantry but the greedy fucker kept clawing the door open to help himself whenever he wanted, so now I have to keep it out of reach. I set his bowl down on the floor in front of him and grab myself an ice pack from the freezer, planning on heading back upstairs to sleep it off, but then movement to my left catches my attention and I stop, turning my head to find my mother raiding the wine rack for a bottle of red.

"Hey, Mom." I tip my chin, sighing when I catch the tick in her jaw. "Aren't you supposed to be on set today?"

She ignores me and sets a glass down on the kitchen counter, avoiding my eyes while she fills it all the way to the top. She's wearing a black pair of leggings and an oversized t-shirt, her long brunette hair tied up in a half assed ponytail on the top of her head. She's beautiful on the outside, tall and slim with a toned body most forty six year old moms would kill for, but on the inside, she's a broken shell of the woman she used to be.

And who's fault is that, dipshit?

My father's cruel words hit me where it hurts and I clear my throat, not liking this awkward tension filling the air between us. Something's up, and it doesn't take a genius to figure out that the answer to my question is no, she's not working today.

"Mom?" I try again, craning my neck in an attempt to catch her eyes. "Are you alrigh–"

"We want you out," she croaks, her shoulders dropping like she's been dying to get the words off her chest.

I blink at that, slowly looking over my shoulder to find my dad standing behind me in the kitchen doorway. His dark gaze travels over my beat up face and he glares, not even bothering to hide his disappointment at the son who ruins everything.

"You know," I state the obvious, nodding to myself when he says nothing. "How did you find out?"

He cocks his head at me and I pull my brows in, but then it hits me and I let out a humourless laugh.

Fucking Felicia.

I ought to steal her walking stick.

"You think this is funny?"

"No," I mutter, leaning back against the island to glance between the two. "You're really kicking me out?"

"God, you've taken it too far this time, Xan," my mom cries, swallowing the last of her wine before pouring herself another one. "We can't keep living like this."

"Like *what*?" I ask, rolling my eyes while I lift the ice pack to my face. "It was a simple misunderstanding, Mom. Mrs Quinn already dropped the charges and promised she wouldn't tell the principal so long as I paid to get it fixed. I didn't get caught by the press. I didn't even get arrested. It's done."

"That's not the point, you idiot!" she snaps, raising her voice in a rare fit of anger. "You stole your teacher's car and wrapped it around a goddamn tree!"

Yeah, well.. I fucked her, too, but I don't tell them that.

"You spent the night in the hospital with a concussion and we had to find out about it from the goddamn *neighbor*," she goes on, quickly swiping her tears away with her hands. "How could you not tell us?"

"Okay, first of all, I didn't steal her car, I *borrowed* it. And this right here is exactly why I didn't tell you. You're a mess, Mom. You need help."

"What I *need* is for my eighteen year old son to start acting like a normal human being and stop risking his life on a daily basis like some kind of adrenaline junkie!" she screams, pushing herself off the counter to shove my chest. "You know damn well how this affects us and yet here you are, still doing the same type of stupid shit that got your brother killed."

The silence that follows stretches for what feels like an eternity and I stay frozen where I stand, unable to move or speak.

She doesn't talk about him.

Not ever.

I've tried a few times over the three years since he's been gone, but she always shuts me down, refusing to remember him.

I remember him.

I remember him for all of us, just like he'd want me to. I kept my fucking promise to him, and if she'd just take the time to listen to me, she'd know that.

"Mom.." I say carefully, stepping closer to run a hand over her shoulder. "I know this isn't gonna make it better, but you have to know I don't do this shit to hurt you. Nik *told* me he didn't want me t–"

She flinches at the sound of his name and shies away from my touch, defensively folding her arms around her body, and fuck if that act alone doesn't crack my damn heart in two. She never touches me anymore, barely even speaks to me unless it's to mutter a half hearted *hello* or *goodbye*, but the worst part of it all is that every time she looks at me, I see the hate in her eyes she barely manages to hide.

Because I'm the reason my big brother is dead, and I don't think she'll ever forgive me for that.

"Go pack your things, Xan," Dad says coolly, leaning back against the wall with his hands shoved into the pockets of his jeans. "I've already spoken to your aunt Karen and finalized your transfer to Lakewood Academy. She's agreed to take you in for the rest of senior year but after that, you're on your own, so I suggest you start looking at colleges and really *think* about what you want to do for the rest of your life, because it sure as hell won't be this."

I nod and run my tongue bar over my teeth, not even bothering to argue with him because judging by the tone of his voice and the look on his face, his mind's already made up and there's no changing it. When Alec Reid wants something, he takes it and makes it happen – something I used to admire about him. I looked up to him for the first fifteen years of my life, respected the shit out of him and strived to be just like him – we *both* did, me and my brother – but now all I see is a cold hearted asshole with the personality of a rock, dead to the world and everyone in it, his wife included.

My parents had one of those epic loves you see in movies – *literally* – they met on the set of this gag worthy romantic suspense back in the nineties and fell hard and fast for each other, but now they can't even stand to be in the same room together.

"I'm taking the dog," I inform him, hitting him with a look that screams *say no, I dare you.*

He was Nik's baby and there's not a chance in hell I'm about to leave him here and let him rot in this soul sucking hole they call a house.

Dad shrugs like he doesn't give a shit and tosses me his collar, leaving to go fuck knows where without so much as a backward glance. "You leave today. Take the jet and buy yourself a new car when you get there."

"Hey, Dad?"

He stops with his hand on the door knob, hesitating a beat before he turns to look at me. "What?"

"You forgot to kiss Mom."

He walks out without biting back and I risk a glance at her, closing my eyes when she grabs her wine and turns her back on me, as well. As soon as she's gone, I clear my throat and look down at the heavy metal chain in my hand, forcing a cocky ass grin despite the solid kick in my heart.

"Come on, buddy," I call, leading the way while he follows me up to my bedroom. "Lakewood's better anyway, right?"

He collapses on the foot of my bed and I shake my head at him, walking through to my closet to grab my suitcase from the shelf overhead.

Right.

2

Jordyn

"You're really not coming?"

"No," my mother sighs, sitting up to remove the thousand dollar sunglasses from her face. "I'm sorry, honey, but you know how hectic these things get. I just can't get away right now."

She's such a liar.

If she were really as *busy* as she says she is, she'd be sitting in a board room right now, not soaking up the rays in some fancy ass hotel in Miami while I sit on the edge of the pool in our back yard, FaceTiming *her* because she can't even be bothered to call me first on my birthday.

I don't dare call her out on it, though.

I never do.

"You promised me you'd be here, Mom," I remind her, keeping my voice low to ensure no one else hears me. "Can't you just come back for tonight and head back out there in the morning?"

"Don't be ridiculous, JJ," she berates me, glancing off to look at something over her shoulder. "You know it doesn't work that way."

In other words, she's found a man. And if history's anything to go by, he's probably a younger man with a sharp jaw and a wallet the size of Texas.

My mother's not a gold digger – she's got enough money to last her a few lifetimes and then some – it's the power and the masculinity she's hot for. My father came out as gay and left her for another guy when I was five, something that hit her self esteem more than she cares to admit. She's been married and divorced three times since then, claiming she falls in love at the drop of a hat, but I know better.

She's terrified of being alone.

She seems to forget that she has *me*, but again, I don't bother calling her out on it.

"What is that you're drinking?"

"It's just soda," I tell her, lifting my glass so she can see.

"You mean *diet* soda, right?"

My jaw ticks but I refrain from saying what I want to say, forcing a grin I don't feel because it's easier than the alternative. "Of course, Mom,"

Her eyes narrow but thankfully she drops it, twirling a long strand of blonde hair around her forefinger while she looks off at something in the distance.

I look so much like her it's almost freaky, but our personalities couldn't be more different. She's driven by money and status, constantly grappling for more of each, and I'm just Elizabeth James' obedient daughter, sole heiress to the Elizabeth James estate and everything that comes with it.

Lucky me.

"When are you coming home?"

"I'm not sure yet," she answers. "Tomorrow, maybe."

"*Maybe?*"

"Yes, *maybe*," she fires back, rolling her eyes when she catches the look on my face. "What is wrong with you? Most girls your age would kill to have a mansion to themselves for their eighteenth birthday. Wouldn't you rather spend your night with Noah?"

"Not really," I mutter, dropping my eyes to play with the yellow strings of my bikini bottoms.

She perks up at that, suddenly interested in me and what I have to say. "Why not?"

I shrug and look off to the house on my right, watching my lifelong boyfriend while he makes himself a drink at the kitchen island. He's got sandy blond hair and bright blue eyes, his navy blue designer swim shorts hanging low on his hips in a way that makes him look hot as hell. He's gorgeous in a pretty boy type of way, but that doesn't change the fact that he's an egotistical dick who thinks he owns me and the ground I walk on.

He doesn't *own* me, and I don't want him to.

Not anymore.

Just as I think it, his eyes hit mine and he narrows them into slits, laughing lightly when my best friend bumps his hip to get him to move out of the way. Penelope flicks her chocolate brown hair over her shoulder and smirks at whatever he's saying to her, shamelessly moving her eyes over his bare chest and abs. He smirks back at the attention and leans back against the counter beside her, boldly returning the favor despite the fact I'm sitting right here.

"JJ?"

"He's not the same anymore, Mom," I whisper, hesitating a second before I decide to elaborate. "He's distant and selfish and he doesn't *care* like he used t–"

"Nonsense," she cuts in, waving me off as if I'm ridiculous for even thinking such a thing. "That boy's been the love of your life since before you could walk. You were made for each other, sweetheart."

I disagree, but just as I open my mouth to plead my case, she shakes her head and raises a hand, done with me and this conversation, apparently.

"Go back inside and work it out with him," she orders, hitting me with a look that screams *do as you're told and smile while you're at it.* "I'll be home as soon as I can and we'll have a spa day together, okay?"

"Mom."

"I have to go, JJ," she sighs. "I'll call you later."

"Okay," I say weakly, struggling to keep the tears at bay. "Bye, Mom."

She hangs up on me and I swallow, pulling my feet out of the water to slide my heels up to my ass. I rest my forearms on my knees and hang my head, silently counting backwards from twenty while I attempt to calm my wounded heart.

Poor, sad little rich girl.

How cliché.

I roll my eyes at the thought and shake it off, reluctantly pushing myself up to walk back inside. I toss my phone down on the kitchen island and open the fridge, ignoring Noah's judgy little eyes on my ass while I pour myself another soda. I suck my stomach in the way my mom taught me to do when I was nine and turn around, pulling out the bar stool beside him to take a seat.

"*Well..*" Penelope draws out, dropping down on my other side to toss a grape into her mouth. "What did she say?"

"She's not coming."

She sticks her bottom lip out and wraps her arm around my neck, scooting over to pull my head down on her shoulder. "I'm sorry, sweetie."

I shrug her off and look up at the monitor in the corner of the room, frowning when I spot the black van pulling up on my driveway. "Who's that?"

"Oh, it's the party people." Penelope grins, jumping up to hold a hand out to Noah. "You got the cash, babe?"

My skin crawls at the endearment but I hide it with a sip of my drink, side eyeing him while she skips off through the house to answer my front door. "You're throwing a party?"

"Is that a problem?"

"No, but I wasn't even supposed to be here tonight," I remind him, laughing lightly when it hits me. "You knew my mom wouldn't show up, didn't you?"

He sighs at that, slowly turning my chair until I'm forced to face him fully. Instead of answering my question, he dips his head and presses his mouth to mine, squeezing my jaw with his fingers when I make no move to kiss him back.

"For fuck's sake, JJ, it's your birthday," he hisses, speaking through his teeth. "Can't you at least *pretend* to be happy for five fucking minutes instead of bringing everyone else down with you?"

I smack his hand from my face and he pulls his head back in surprise, looking up over my shoulder when a throat clears from somewhere behind me.

"The alcohol's heavy," Penelope informs him, feigning awkwardness when all she wants to do is laugh. "Can you come help me carry it inside?"

He nods and looks back to me, brushing a loose strand of hair behind my ear in a way that's more threatening than sweet. "Go take a shower and fix your hair the way I like it," he orders. "It looks better when you curl it."

I keep my mouth shut and he kisses my forehead, stealing my drink to pour it into the sink on his way out. My eyes burn with unshed tears but I force myself to smile at him, partly because I'm not about to let them see me cry but mostly because I'm Jordyn fucking James, and I have nothing to be sad about.

3

Xander

Aunt Karen takes one look at me and scrunches her nose, blatantly moving her disapproving gaze over me and my form while I jump out of the car I bought just now. My dad said I could get whatever I wanted so I chose Nik's dream car – a black on black Chevy Camaro with chrome wheels and a badass leather interior. I would've bought one before now, but my mom already hates me enough. I didn't want to piss her off even more by buying something that would remind her of her dead son every time she saw me pull up outside.

My lazy ass dog refuses to move from the passenger seat so I give him a little tug, laughing lightly when I catch the look of horror on Karen's face.

"He's really good, I swear."

"He better be," she says, walking down the front steps to hand me a set of keys.

She's wearing a white formal pantsuit and black heels, her dark brown hair pulled into a flawless bun at the nape of her neck. Her entire demeanour screams *don't fuck with me*, and I won't deny I'm a little bit scared of her. I don't know her that well considering she and my mom had a huge fight just before she moved to LA to chase her dreams of becoming an actress twenty eight years ago, but what I do know is that she's a take no shit type of girl who just so happens to be the principal of Lakewood Academy – one of the top private schools in the country and the place I'm about to spend five days a week at for the next seven months.

"Still not a hugger, huh?" I joke, awkwardly rolling my lips when I realize she doesn't find me funny.

"You're staying in the pool house," she informs me, straight down to business, as usual. "Clean sheets and towels are stored in the linen closet next to the bathroom. Don't stay out all night without calling me first and do not break the law. While you're living under my roof you will clean up after yourself and keep your grades up. I am your principal and your guardian until you graduate this summer, not your maid or your get out of jail free card. Do I make myself clear?"

"Yes ma'am."

Seemingly satisfied with my response, she nods and turns around to walk back inside, leaving me alone to see myself in. I shake my head at her and grab my shit from the trunk, walking around the side of her house to get to the pool house at the back. It's a modern, one story building with gray stone walls and wooden finishes, a wide set of four steps leading up to the sliding glass doors covering the entire front wall. There's a huge bed made up on the back wall with two matching nightstands either side of it, two wooden doors that I assume lead to a separate bathroom and the linen closet she mentioned just now, a fully stocked kitchen on my left, and a sunken living room with a corner couch and a flat screen TV on my right.

Bear immediately jumps up onto the bed to claim his rightful spot and I grin, lifting my suitcase up off the floor to drop it down beside him. I open it up and take out the photo frame I stashed beneath one of my hoodies to keep it safe, carefully running my thumb over the glass covering my brother's face. This is the last one I took of us together – my arm wrapped around his inked neck while he flips me off through the front facing camera on my phone.

"Damn, boy, you got big."

I raise a brow at that, glancing over my shoulder to find Travis standing behind me dressed in a pair of gym shorts and a tight t-shirt. I've only met my cousin twice in person – once when our grandmother died when we were seven and once again when Nik died three years ago – but we've kept in touch over the years through Instagram and FaceTime and shit.

"You talkin' to me or the dog?"

"The dog, dipshit," he fires back, stepping closer to bump my fist with his. "They kicked you out, huh?"

I nod and set my picture down on the nightstand, grabbing a few shirts from my case to hang them up inside the free standing closet on my right.

"What'd you do this time?"

"Crashed my teacher's car."

"Of course you did," he mutters, gesturing to my face with a flick of his wrist. "What happened there?"

"I fucked this college girl last night and she hit me, then her big brother picked her up and hit me, as well."

He snorts and hops up onto the kitchen counter, side eyeing Bear every few seconds like he's afraid he's about to jump up and eat him.

"You can touch him if you want," I offer, gently scratching the spot beneath his chin. "He won't bite."

"I'm good, thanks."

I laugh and continue unpacking my shit, chewing the inside of my cheek when my aunt's raised voice rings out in the distance. She's arguing with my uncle, and I don't miss the words *your delinquent nephew* and *disaster waiting to happen* leaving his mouth. An awkward silence stretches between us and Travis clears his throat, shrugging it off like it's nothing.

"It's not you, man," he says, sighing while he runs a hand through his dark brown hair. "Last night they had a bust up over a broken lightbulb. I swear they pick fights out of thin air just to get a rise out of each other."

Their screaming match gets louder and I close the doors, moving for the fridge beside him to grab a couple bottles of water. "At least your parents still care enough to argue," I mutter, passing him one before I sit down to uncap my own. "Mine don't even talk to each other anymore."

He nods, looking over at the picture on my nightstand, and I can tell he wants to say something about Nik. He doesn't, of course, but fuck, I wish he would. I wish people would grow some fucking balls and stop treating my brother's name like it's a dirty curse word set out to offend, but I'm not naïve enough to believe that's about to happen any time soon.

Death makes people uncomfortable.

That's just the way it is.

"You wanna stay in and order a pizza?" he asks, tipping his chin at the big screen in the corner. "Grab some beers and watch a movie or some shit?"

I frown at that, pulling my head back to emphasise my outrage. "It's Saturday, Trav."

"Yeah, so?"

"So where's the party at?"

I pull up outside some big ass mansion a little while later and Travis releases the breath he's been holding, only just letting go of the *oh shit* handle to drop his head back on the seat. "I'm never getting in a car with you again."

I laugh at him and kill the ignition, jumping out of the driver's seat to fall in line beside him. "Who the hell lives here?" I ask, side eyeing the six square shaped pillars out front and the full on water fountain set up in the middle of the driveway. "The president?"

"Don't be a dick," he chuckles, pushing the front door open to let himself inside. "Her name's Jordyn but we call her JJ. She's Elizabeth James' daughter."

I nod and look around, frowning when he eyes me like he's expecting a bigger reaction than my non existent one. "What?"

"*Elizabeth James*, Xan," he draws out, walking me across the massive entryway and through to the kitchen. "The designer chick with all the fur coats and the dresses and the shoes? *That's* who lives here."

"Fuck off."

"I'm dead serious," he laughs, grabbing two shot glasses and a bottle of vodka from the island. "I've known them since kindergarten."

Well, shit.

He pours our drinks and I look around again, confused and a little put out by the vibe in here. The high school kids where I'm from spend their weekends on stained couches in grungy basements, smoking weed and licking cocaine from their fingertips while getting their dicks sucked by hot girls who have no problem getting their tits out for all to see.

These people don't play like that.

This house is immaculate and white and.. *sterile*. No one's smoking inside or yelling or breaking shit. No one's throwing punches in a fit of drunken rage or fucking on the staircase. Instead they're all wearing designer dresses and clean shirts, drinking expensive liquor from pink plastic cups and grinding on each other in a way that's more hot than disgusting.

"Is it always like this?"

"Pretty much, yeah." Travis nods, passing me a shot glass to knock it with his.

We throw them back and he tilts his head for me to follow him, easily moving through this maze of a house like he's been here a thousand times before. He introduces me to a colourful looking guy with blonde hair and I bump his fist, raising a brow when he moves his eyes over my form like he's fixing to eat me.

"Kian," Travis says, speaking through his teeth.

"What?"

"He's not gay."

"Really?" He frowns, looking genuinely confused by that. "Honey, you look a little gay."

"Yeah, I get that a lot."

"I'll bet," he muses, still checking me out despite the

solid glare on the side of his face.

I hide a grin and run a hand over the back of my neck, looking up at the curved staircase when a flash of wavy blonde hair steals my attention.

"That's JJ," Travis informs me, laughing lightly when he catches the look on my face.

He carries on talking but I don't hear him because *fuck me*, Jordyn James is *fine*. She's got long hair cut down to the curve of her back and a body built for sin, her tiny waist and round ass wrapped up in a black strapless dress I wouldn't mind peeling off with my teeth. Her hips sway with every step she takes and she smiles politely at the group of girls at the bottom, but I don't miss the way it looks a little.. forced.

She belongs in a place like this the same way sharks belong in the ocean – that much is clear – but she also looks like she'd rather be a million miles away.

Bored.

Happy but not happy.

Here but not *here*.

"Don't even think about it, Xan," Travis warns, but it's a little too late for that.

I'm already thinking about it, picturing myself shoving her down on her back, having her look up at me from beneath those thick lashes of hers while I push her dress up over her ass and sink my cock into her pussy.

"Dude, she's got a boyfriend," Travis says, tipping his chin at yet another blond guy who looks like a pretty boy douchebag. "That's Noah Campbell, the mayor's son. They've been together since they were kids."

"Is that right?" I mutter, unable to take my eyes off her

while Noah steps up to block her path at the bottom of the stairs.

He glares at her and I glare at him, watching him while he hisses words out through his teeth and waves a hand over her form like there's something wrong with her.

There's *nothing* wrong with her, the stupid fucker.

She's fucking flawless.

"Xan, she's *taken*," my cousin stresses. "And even if she wasn't, she's not that type of girl. She'd never go for someone like you."

"The fuck's that supposed to mean?"

"You know exactly what it means," he laughs, clapping a hand down on my shoulder to guide me away from her. "You're the guy who'll fuck her once and ruin her life just to ignore her for the rest of yours."

I smirk and slide my eyes back to the princess, still picturing the way those sexy black heels are gonna look wrapped around my waist. "Hey, Trav?"

"What?"

"Do you dare me?"

He shakes his head at that, knowing I'll do pretty much anything I'm told when it comes to the game. It's the reason for all this purple shit in my hair and the ink covering my skin and the piercings on my body.

It's the reason my brother is dead.

"You're a real piece of shit sometimes, you know that?"

I nod and pour myself another drink at the kitchen island, looking over again to find Jordyn turning away from Noah to walk back upstairs. Some dark haired girl appears at his side a few seconds later and I knock Travis' arm with my elbow, tipping my chin at them.

"Who's the girl?"

"Penelope Sanchez," he answers. "JJ's best friend."

I raise a brow at that, not missing the way the so called *best friend* moves in further to rest a hand on Noah's chest. He leans over to say something in her ear and I click my tongue at him, shamelessly grinning to myself while I lean back against the counter to neck my shot.

This'll be easier than I thought.

ND# Little Devil

4

Jordyn

Go change, he says.

This dress makes you look like a slut, he says.

I slam my bedroom doors behind me and grit my teeth, folding my arms behind my back to work the zipper down. It gets stuck three times where I'm so agitated with myself, but I finally get the stupid dress off and toss it into the corner of my closet, walking over to the rail on the back wall to grab the white one he demanded I wear instead.

You're asking for it, he says.

What an asshole.

I should go down there and tell him to go fuck himself, tell him I'm no one's goddamn *property* and I can wear whatever the hell I want, fuck him and his opinion.

I don't do that, though.

Instead I pull on the outfit he chose *for me* and switch my heels out for a strappy nude pair, turning around to face free standing mirror set up in the corner. It's a skin tight, long sleeved dress with a cleavage cut out showing the top halves of my breasts and a little bit of thigh, but not too much. *Sexy but elegant*, my mother called it when she designed it for me a few weeks ago.

Whatever.

I run my fingers through my curls and plaster a smile on my face, forcing myself to head back down to the party I never wanted. I find Noah standing in the entryway with a couple of the boys from school and head over there, not so patiently waiting for him to finish talking before I open my mouth to speak.

"Better?" I ask, hoping he doesn't notice the sarcasm lacing my tone.

"Beautiful," he says quietly, leaning over me to kiss my forehead. "Go have some fun. I'll find you in a little bit."

For sex, he means.

He'll find me for sex.

I bite back a scoff and walk away from him, passing a bunch of people I see almost every day but don't talk to. I grab a cup from the kitchen island and make myself a vodka soda – full fat, because fuck everybody – rolling my eyes when I spot Penelope and Sienna talking shit to Alyssa Rose, the mousy haired new girl who failed to hide the fact she had a little crush on Noah when she first got here at the beginning of senior year. She doesn't like him anymore – she realized pretty quickly what a self centred piece of shit he really is – but it seems my friends don't feel like letting it go just yet.

"You're not welcome here, loser."

"Noah doesn't want you."

"He'll *never* want a cheap whore like you."

I do scoff this time. Loudly.

Fucking please, Penelope.

"Hey, Alyssa?" I call, tilting my head at the patio doors leading to the back yard. "Grace was looking for you outside just now. I think she's pretty out of it."

She offers me a grateful smile and I wink at her, raising a brow at the girls when they hit me with their pathetic scowls, angry with me for taking away their play thing.

Sienna's mostly harmless – the blonde haired, follow the leader, all bark and no bite type of bully – but Penelope's passive aggressive and toxic – the type of friend who'll tell you how hot you look in a bikini and then make a gag face behind your back.

She won't say shit to me, but I have a feeling that has less to do with our lifelong friendship and more to do with ensuring she stays on my boyfriend's good side.

"We're gonna go do shots with the boys," she tells me, stepping forward to take a bottle of tequila from the island. "Wanna come?"

"Maybe later."

She rolls her eyes at me and I roll mine right back, leaning my elbows on the counter to run a finger over the edge of my cup.

I'm so tired of this shit.

Tired of my mom and Noah treating me like I'm worthless beyond my looks, tired of the parties and my friends and their never ending pissing contest over who's got the biggest house, the richest parents, the flashiest car, the smallest waist..

No one fucking cares.

Little Devil

But even as I think it, I know it's a lie.

That's *all* anyone cares about.

It's pathetic.

It seems I'm just as pathetic as the rest of them, though, because instead of drinking the vodka soda I made myself just now, I lean over and pour it into the kitchen sink. *21st Century Vampire* by Lil Huddy plays through the surround sound and I smile to myself at the lyrics, moving to grab a diet soda from the fridge. I pop the cap off the top and close the door with my elbow, damn near jumping out of my skin when I connect eyes with a strange looking guy I've never seen before.

"Jesus, fu–" I stop before I embarrass myself further and grab a hand towel from the counter, scrunching my nose while I wipe the soda from my hand and wrist.

He laughs quietly and I glare, crouching down in front of him to clean the mess off the floor. He's leaning back against the wall with his hands shoved into his pockets and his head cocked to the side, his messy hair falling over his eyes in a way that makes him look.. lost?

There's no way he goes to Lakewood.

Or college.

That might be a little stereotypical on my part but *come on*, he's wearing black ripped jeans and a faded black t-shirt, his arms and throat covered in a bunch of tattoos I can't make out in the low lighting. Not only that, his hair is *purple*, for fuck's sake – long, thick strands sticking up in all directions like he messed it up on purpose and left it that way. He's got two silver rings in his nostrils and a diagonal slit in his eyebrow, and I don't miss the nasty looking bruise beneath his left eye or the small cut on the corner of his bottom lip. As if sensing my eyes on it, his tongue slips out to lick the spot and I pull my brows in, oddly fascinated by the flash of metal in his mouth. That same mouth forms a dirty little grin and I lift my eyes up to his, quickly snapping my own mouth shut when I realize he's caught me gawking at him.

Goddamnit.

I straighten up with as much dignity as I can muster and set my soda down on the counter, side eyeing him over my shoulder when I feel him staring at me. I have no idea who he is or who he came here with, but asking him what the hell he thinks he's doing in my house seems a little rude and presumptuous, so I decide on a safer option.

Ignoring him.

"You need some help with that?"

I blink at the sound of his voice behind me, somewhat surprised he said anything. "Excuse me?"

"Your drink," he explains, pushing himself off the wall to move in next to me.

He takes a clean cup from the stack and I frown at the ink on his arms, unsure what to make of him. The way he looks screams troubled loner boy, but the way he moves and handles himself screams fuck me sideways.

He's not horrible to look at, not really, but he's not what I consider hot, either.

Right?

Right.

"You think a lot of words for such a quiet little thing," he says, looking over at me from beneath his dark lashes, and I can't help but note the way he hasn't taken his eyes off me in I don't know how long.

"What makes you think I'm quiet?"

"Lucky guess."

"Or maybe you're stalking me."

"Maybe," he muses, smiling to himself while he hands me my new drink.

I raise a brow and look from him to it and back again, making him laugh. Knowing exactly what I'm thinking, he lifts it to his mouth and takes a sip.

"Happy?"

"Finish it," I offer, reaching over him to take an unopened bottle of vodka from the side. "That way if you did put something in it, *you'll* be the one on your ass tonight and it'll serve you right."

He laughs at me again but does as he's told, necking the entire thing in one go before resting his elbows on the counter beside me. "Hey, Jordyn?"

"It's JJ," I correct him, not even bothering to ask how he knows my name when I didn't give it to him yet.

For some reason I'm more interested in what he has to say than interrogating him on his stalking abilities.

"*JJ*," he says mockingly, leaning in even further like he's about to tell me a secret. "Wanna fuck?"

My jaw drops and I pull my head back, amazed and a little speechless at the audacity. "You're joking, right?"

"Not even a little bit."

Jesus Christ.

"I.. I have a boyfriend."

"I have a cat."

I frown at that, scrunching my nose in confusion.

"What does that have to do with anything?"

He smirks, cocky as shit. "Exactly."

It takes me a second, but then it hits me and I gape at him. "Are you serious right now?"

"No," he chuckles, somehow managing to keep a straight face when he adds, "I don't have a cat."

"You're an asshole," I point out, but he just shrugs like he doesn't give a fuck, not at all offended by the fact.

"I know."

"You *know*–"

"Hey, JJ."

I shut my mouth and turn to face my friend Kian, laughing lightly when he takes my hand and lifts it up over my head to spin me around in a circle.

"Gorgeous," he praises, leaning over me to kiss my cheeks. "I see you've met the new boy I can't stop thinking about. He's hot, right?"

"So hot," I deadpan, narrowing my eyes when the *new boy* grins like I'm serious. "You know this guy, Ki?"

"Yeah, that's Xander Reid, Travis' cousin. He just moved here from California. Isn't that great?"

I have nothing to say to that so I say nothing, looking up when I spot Noah headed this way with his arm wrapped around Penelope's waist.

"This one's done for the night," he laughs, reaching over to grab her phone from the counter. "I'm gonna take her up to her room before she passes out."

Yet another forced smile crosses my lips and I watch them leave, ignoring the bile creeping up my throat when he looks down and grins at whatever she's mumbling into his shoulder. Kian clears his throat while he turns around to pour himself another drink and Xander stares at me, moving in to retake his spot at the counter beside me.

"*What?*" I bite out, a little meaner than I intended.

"What?" he laughs, feigning innocence, but I'm not falling for it.

There's nothing *innocent* about him.

Not a damn thing.

"Spit it out, new boy."

He fails to hide his amusement and runs his tongue bar over his teeth, shamelessly moving his eyes over my form like he has the right. "You look hot in white."

"But.." I push, knowing there's more.

"*But..*" he goes on, leaning into me until his lips are just an inch from mine. "The black one suited you better."

My eyes cut to his and he winks at me, backing away to leave me here with my mouth hanging open for the fourth time in ten minutes.

"I dare you to speak your words, Jordyn James."

Make that the fifth time.

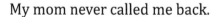

My mom never called me back.

Never even sent me a text to let me know she was too busy to talk.

She forgot about me, just like she always does.

I sigh and lie back on the cushioned porch swing outside, enjoying the view of the ocean beneath the black sky in the distance. This little corner of the world is close enough to the city that you can grab whatever you need within an hour, but far enough away that you can actually see the stars in the sky.

It's beautiful down there.

Picture worthy.

My phone buzzes in my hand and I immediately look down at it, rolling my eyes at myself when I realize it's not my mother, just an Instagram notification. My feed is full of pictures and stories from the party tonight, a few of the people from school tagging me in their posts to wish me a happy birthday. I scroll through and stop when I get to the video Sienna tagged me in a little while ago. She's posing in front of the camera with a pink shot glass in her hand and a few of the boys either side of her, but that's not what I'm looking at. Noah's standing in the corner behind them with his hands on Penelope's hips, playfully shaking his head at whatever she's saying to him. She runs her hands over his chest and he looks around to check no one's looking, then he leans over her and teases her lips with his.

Jesus.

My eyes water and I look up at Penelope's balcony, wincing at the sting when I catch them in her bedroom together. He's got her pinned up against the glass with her legs wrapped around his waist and his mouth on her neck, squeezing her ass with one hand while he tears the dress from her body with the other.

So much for her being *done for the night.*

I swear to god they think I'm stupid, but then maybe I

am stupid for ignoring my gut for so long.

You always knew, JJ.

Embarrassment courses through me and I swallow the lump in my throat, hesitating a second while I decide what to do. I don't usually like confrontation – I'd rather dissolve conflict than be the one to create it – but something inside me has me feeling brave tonight.

I dare you to speak your words, Jordyn James.

I stand up before I can talk myself out of it and walk back inside the house, ignoring everyone and everything around me while I move through the crowd like a zombie on autopilot. I get up to the second floor and enter my bedroom, grabbing the spare key for Penelope's room from my nightstand – the same room I gave her a couple years ago to ensure she always has a safe place to hook up whenever she needs it.

Fucking figures she's using it to hook up with *my* boyfriend right under my nose, but there you have it.

I make my way to the end of the hall and stop just outside her bedroom door, taking a minute to get my nerves in check before I move to unlock it. I walk inside and Penelope squeals from her spot on the bed beneath Noah, quickly snatching a pillow from the headboard to cover her naked body. Noah jumps up to shove his cock back into his jeans and Penelope slaps a hand over her mouth, only just realizing it's me, it seems.

"Oh, shit."

Yeah. Shit.

She opens her mouth like she's about to try and explain her way out of it but I shake my head to stop her, not even a little bit interested in whatever she has to say.

"Get out."

"JJ, please, just let m–"

"I said *get out*," I repeat, tilting my head at the door to dismiss her. "Now."

She swallows and leans over to grab her dress from the floor, awkwardly throwing it on over her head before she moves to do as she's told. She scurries off through the door and I look at Noah, laughing lightly when I catch the regret on his face, but I don't find him funny.

"JJ, listen–"

"No, I won't liste–"

"But it's not what you thin–"

"Shut the fuck up!" I shout, effectively shocking him into silence. "Jesus, Noah, what the hell is the matter with you? You said you'd *find me later*, remember? How many times have you fucked my best friend and left her here just to come back and fuck me an hour later?"

He scrubs a hand over his mouth and moves forward like he's about to touch me, frowning in confusion when I take a step back to get away from him.

"*No.*"

"What?"

"Don't come near me."

"JJ.."

Silent tears spill over my cheeks and I curse myself for crying in front of him, but they're not sad tears. They're tears of anger and betrayal and..

Jesus, is that relief?

That crushing weight I've been carrying around for months now finally eases up some and I release the breath I've been holding, dipping my head as discreetly as I can to wipe my eyes with my fingers.

"Damn it, JJ, please don't get upset."

"I'm not upset, Noah," I say quietly, backing up towards the door with my hands raised. "I'm just done."

"What do you mean, you're *done*?"

"I mean I'm done," I repeat, unsure how I can make this any clearer for him. "*We're* done."

"JJ, wait–"

But I don't wait.

Instead I turn around and head back downstairs, not missing the way almost every person I pass has their phone in their hand and their eyes on me.

Word got out fast, it seems.

I pretend they don't exist and grab my car keys from the kitchen, inwardly rolling my eyes when I spot Sienna comforting Penelope while she cries into her hands in the corner. Noah's raised voice rings out from somewhere behind me and I slip out through the front door, freezing where I stand when I run right into Xander Reid on the front steps.

Shit.

He cocks his head at me and inhales a hit of his cigarette, casually craning his neck to get a look at the commotion behind me. "What are you running fro–"

"I spoke my words," I blurt out, immediately feeling stupid for saying it when he was probably just messing with me, but he doesn't make me feel stupid.

His brows jump in surprise and he bounces his eyes between mine, searching for I don't know what, then he runs his thumb over his lip to hide a grin and steps aside to move out of the way. I blow out a breath and make a beeline for my car, quickly tossing my heels over to the passenger seat before I jump inside. I hit the gas and drive down to the beach a couple miles away, pulling up at the back of the empty parking lot to grab my camera bag from the glove compartment. Leaving my heels behind, I walk down to the shoreline and take out my Nikon, carefully twisting the lens to zoom in on the stars in the distance.

Like I said.. beautiful.

Little Devil

5

Xander

She's fucking amazing.

A pretty little princess who drives a pristine white Tesla to match her disgustingly pristine life, but still amazing all the same.

I didn't think she'd *actually* do it, didn't think she'd have the nerve to stand up to that douchebag boyfriend of hers and the girl she calls a best friend, but here we are.

She fucking *did it*.

All because I dared her to.

I probably don't deserve all the credit for her little outburst tonight – that was all her – but I won't deny the twisted thrill rushing through me at the fact I played at least a part in the unravelling of this epic shit show.

Penelope's still sobbing in the kitchen with some blonde chick I think is Sienna, Travis and Kian are swallowing shot after shot with their heads hung low, looking sheepish and guilty as fuck, and Noah's still searching this big ass house from top to bottom, still looking for the girl who got the fuck out of here the first chance she got.

I should probably tell him she left, be the *good guy* my mother raised me to be and put him out of his misery, but it's more enjoyable for me to watch him seethe like an angry toddler who's gone and lost his favorite toy.

"Where the fuck *is* she?" he growls, spinning in a half circle to glare at Sienna for the third time in ten minutes. "This is all your fault, you know?"

"*My* fault?"

"Yes, *your* fault," he grits out, lifting his phone to show her the video she posted on Instagram earlier tonight. "If you weren't such an attention seeking slut she'd have never caught me up there."

"Dude." Travis shakes his head, sighing when Noah slides his glare this way. "Just.. sit your ass down and chill out for a sec, yeah? You're acting crazy."

"I don't give a fuck!" he shouts, throwing his hands out to emphasise his rage. "My girl is *gone*, you idiot. What the fuck am I supposed to do?"

"Maybe try keeping your dick out of her best friend," I offer, shrugging while I finish the last of my drink. "See if that makes a difference."

Several pairs of eyes pop wide in shock and Noah pulls his head back, gesturing to me with a thumb thrown over his shoulder. "Who the fuck is this freak?"

I cock my head at him and my cousin looks at me, raising a brow with a look that says *aren't you gonna tell them?* He's probably expecting me to sit here and brag about who my parents are, but I've got something better to brag about. Smug as fuck, I stand and place my empty cup down on the kitchen island, stepping closer to the *boyfriend* until our noses are just a few inches apart.

"I'm the freak who's gonna steal your girl."

His nostrils flare and Travis closes his eyes, dropping his head to pinch the bridge of his nose. "Fucking hell, Xan."

I laugh lightly and shove my hands into my pockets, backing away from Noah to tilt my head at the front door. "You comin', Trav?"

"Yeah," he sighs, pushing himself off the counter to toss a half hearted wave at his friends.

They mumble their goodbyes and he follows me outside, snatching the keys from my hand with a drunken shake of his head.

"What?"

"I wasn't kidding earlier," he says, bypassing my car to tip his chin at the road up ahead. "It's not that far. I'll give you a ride to get your car in the morning."

I shrug and fall in line to start walking, not missing the obvious slump in his shoulders or the way he won't stop running his hands over his face.

"What's wrong with you?"

"Nothing," he mutters, rolling his eyes when I hit him with my best *I call bullshit* look. "I just feel bad for JJ, man. I mean, it's bad enough finding out you're being cheated on, but to catch them on her birthday in front of almost everyone she knows.. it fucking sucks."

Wait..

"It's her *birthday*?"

He nods and I frown, turning my head to glance back at the direction she drove off in earlier.

Fuck.

6

Jordyn

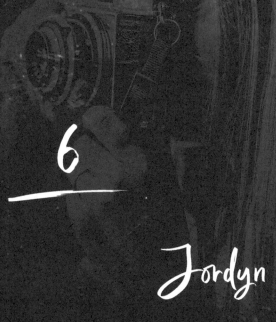

A loud, persistent knocking sound echoes through my bedroom and I groan, blindly reaching for my pillow to bury my head beneath it.

Go away.

"Come in," I call, feigning a cheerfulness I don't feel.

The double doors open and a heavy sigh fills my ears, followed by a thick British accent that grates on my nerves. "Why aren't you up yet?"

"Because it's Sunday," I mutter, rolling my eyes when she taps her stiletto against the floor beneath her feet, impatiently waiting for me to show my face.

Maryanne's a beautiful woman in her early forties – tall and slim with a gorgeous head of thick, black hair. She's been with us for as long as I can remember, practically raised me herself thanks to my absent mother and her love for work and men, but that doesn't change the fact that she's a massive pain in my ass.

"There's someone at the door for you," she informs me, lifting a defensive hand when she catches the glare on my face. "It's not Noah. We're all very aware you told us not to bother you if he showed up here today. It's someone else. Another boy."

"What boy?"

"I don't know," she sighs, moving for the patio doors on the north wall to fling the curtains open. "Come downstairs and see to your.. *visitor*. And for goodness sake, put some clothes on. Your mother would have a fit if she saw you walking around dressed like that."

I flip her off behind her back and stand up to grab my white robe from the floor, throwing the cool silk over my shoulders to cover the short pyjama shorts and cropped tank top I'm wearing. I make my way down to the front door and swing it open, pulling my head back when I find Xander Reid standing on my front steps in the exact same spot as last night, only he's not smoking a cigarette this time. His eyes widen a little bit when he sees what I'm wearing and he curses, blatantly checking me out from head to toe.

"My eyes are up here," I point out, crossing my arms over my chest to hide my body from him.

"Yeah, but your *ass* is down *there*."

I drop my jaw at that, honest to god wondering if he was dropped a lot as a kid. "You're.."

"I'm *what*?"

"Disgusting," I decide. "You're disgusting."

A real life grin spreads across his stupid face and he dips his head, glancing up at me from beneath his lashes in a way that'd make him look hot as fuck if he didn't irritate me so much.

"What do you want, new boy?"

"Me and Trav are gonna go grab some breakfast at Lucky's," he tells me, tilting his head at his cousin's car parked behind the Camaro on my driveway.

Travis offers me a nervous smile from his spot in the drivers seat and I reluctantly smile back, working my jaw when I catch the look on his face. It's pity, and I don't miss the way he can barely look me in the eye after what happened here last night.

"You wanna come?" Xander asks, purposely ignoring the tension between me and his cousin.

"No."

"Why not?"

Because all my so called friends will be there and I don't have the courage to face them right now. I'm fully aware I'll have to see them at school tomorrow, but this is *my* day – the one day I'm giving myself to wallow in my own self pity until it's time to face the music.

I don't tell him any of that, though.

Instead I keep my mouth shut and take a second to look at him, *really* look at him for the first time since I opened the door just now. He's wearing yet another pair of ripped jeans and a black t-shirt, his purple hair still a little damp from the shower he must have taken before coming here. His eyes are hazel, I only just notice, so light they almost look gold in the light of day. They're annoyingly gorgeous and magnetic, and I can't help but wonder how he'd look on the other side of my camera, leaning back against the Camaro I'm not sure how he can afford, his hands shoved into his pockets with his head cocked to the side, that cocky little smirk on his face that makes me want to punch him..

Fucking sexy.

That's how he'd look.

"What's with the hair?"

He raises a brow and I blush before I can stop it, inwardly cursing myself for asking that out loud.

"It was a dare," he says simply, shrugging like that explains it. "You like it?"

"I.." I consider lying to him but decide against it, knowing it'll boost his already massive ego but telling him anyway. "I don't hate it."

He laughs lightly at that. "Thank you."

"You're welcome. Now go away."

"Go out with me tonight."

My hand freezes on the door knob and I turn around to face him, scrunching my nose when I realize he's not messing with me. "What?"

"Go out with me tonight," he repeats, slower this time. "No Travis. Just me and you."

I blink, then I blink again, blinking several times while my brain attempts to process his stupidity. "You're asking me out on a *date*?"

"Yep."

"Okay, let me rephrase that. You're asking me out on a date less than twelve hours after I broke up with my boyfriend for fucking my best friend?"

He grins that stupid grin again. "Yep."

I slam the door in his face and flick the lock, heading for the kitchen to go find myself some breakfast. "Asshole."

I pause the movie I'm watching by myself and wrap my arms around my waist, leaning my head back on the twelve seater couch to glare at the huge, cinema style big screen on the front wall of the den.

This is beyond pathetic.

I've got everything a girl could ask for, always have and probably always will, and yet I don't think I've ever felt this sad in my life.

Embarrassed and stupid and *alone.*

A defeated sigh leaves me and I wipe my eyes with my sleeves, standing up from my seat in search of some chocolate and ice cream. We don't keep that stuff here, of course, so I grab my phone despite the fact it's been switched off since last night and head out to my car, frowning when I spot the white envelope attached to my windshield. I walk around to the front and pick it off, squinting into the darkness to read the unfamiliar handwriting scribbled across the back of it.

Jordyn.

"What the fuck?" I whisper to myself, quickly glancing left and right to check for movement.

Finding nothing but my own driveway and the trees surrounding it, I shake off that stupid glimmer of hope in my chest and flip it over to tear it open.

My dad's the only person who calls me Jordyn, but there's no way he would leave this here, not after all this time without a word..

Something falls from the card and I scramble to catch

it with my left hand, quickly looking around again before I turn it over to inspect it. It's a keychain, a purple one in the shape of that smirking devil emoji Kian uses all the time. Still confused, I open the only birthday card I got this year and read the note written on the inside.

Smile, princess.

There's always next year.

7

Xander

I pull up beside Travis in the parking lot and climb out of my car, desperately tugging on the air stealing leash around my neck while I look up at my new school. Lakewood Academy is just as I imagined it would be – a modern style building crawling with superficial rich kids. It's admittedly not *that* much different to the public school I went to in LA – they were all rich assholes, too, myself included – but at least we didn't have to wear these stupid ass uniforms there.

Travis looks my way and rolls his eyes, snatching the cigarette from my mouth to toss it on the ground.

"Hey."

"Dude, knock it off," he hisses, snatching my forearm to pull me towards the steps leading up to the main entrance. "My mom'll kill you if she catches you smoking out here."

"Why are you so worried?"

"I'm not worried," he lies, sighing when I raise a brow at him. "It's nothing. Just.. keep your head down and stay away from Noah, yeah?"

"Why?"

"Oh, I don't know," he deadpans. "Maybe because you told him you were gonna steal his girlfriend in front of half the fucking school."

I laugh at that, still tugging on the knot around my neck while I follow him inside. "You have to admit that was kinda funny."

"It wasn't funny."

It was, but whatever.

He walks me to my locker and I unlock it with the combination his mom gave me at breakfast this morning. She didn't look very happy with me and my appearance, but instead of going off on me like I expected her to, she kept her judgy little opinion to herself and handed me my schedule, warning me to behave myself or else.

I'm really not looking forward to finding out whatever *or else* means.

Kian appears at my side and I bump his fist, chuckling when he wraps his arm around my neck and walks me to class. "You sure you're not gay, Xander Reid?"

"Positive."

"Shame," he teases, reaching up to run a hand through my hair. "I'd look hot as fuck with your dick in my ass."

"*Kian*," Travis growls, making him jump.

"What?"

"Get off him."

"Jealous much?" he jokes, earning himself yet another glare from my usually chill cousin.

I frown at the obvious tension between them and round the corner, damn near tripping over my own feet when I spot Jordyn James walking through the double doors at the other end of the hall. She's wearing a white button down tucked neatly into a black and white checkered skirt, her Lakewood Academy tie wrapped perfectly around her neck in a way that makes me wanna pull on it. Her heels echo against the tiled floor while she walks through the parted crowd with her eyes on her phone, doing a helluva good job to ignore the eyes following her every move. Most of the students lingering on the sidelines are all pointing and whispering shit with their heads in close, but the princess pretends not to notice, discreetly rolling her eyes when Sienna scurries to keep up with her.

"Dude, will you quit staring at her?" Travis whispers, knocking my elbow with his when I refuse to take my eyes off her. "It's creepy."

He's probably right, but I can't help it.

Something about her just *calls* to me in a way I've never experienced before.

She looks so put together and fake and trapped and so fucking hot I can't stand it.

She looks like mine.

"JJ, wait!" Noah calls, pulling me from my thoughts.

She stops to open her locker and he glares at Sienna, effectively dismissing her without a word. She moves to stand beside Travis and Kian and Noah leans in to say something to Jordyn, not noticing the way her tiny little hands curl into fists around her books. She looks like she wants to go off on him, and fuck, I wish she would, but instead of punching him in the mouth, she forces that stupid smile and says something I can't hear, then she side steps him and walks into class without looking back. Noah's eyes immediately hit mine and he locks his jaw, glaring again when he catches the look on my face.

"The fuck are you staring at, *freak*?" he bites out, loud enough for all to hear.

"You've got lip gloss on your mouth," I inform him, stepping closer to bump his shoulder with mine. "Clean it up, asshole."

Penelope walks around the corner wearing the same fucking shade of cherry red and I walk into first period, winking at Jordyn when I catch her standing just inside the door with her head turned over her shoulder and her mouth parted. Her brows pull in and she moves her eyes over my disheveled uniform, shaking her head at me with a small smile on her lips – a *real* fucking smile – before taking her seat at the back of the class. I hide my grin and move for the teacher's desk, finding a hot brunette woman in her mid to late twenties with her thin glasses perched on the edge of her nose.

"Hi, I'm–"

"Xander Reid, the principal's nephew," she finishes for me, not looking up while she scribbles something on her notepad. "Can you be trusted to sit with your cousin without disrupting my class?"

"Yes, ma'am."

She nods and rips the paper off, handing it to me with a tip of her chin. "Sit down and turn to page thirty one."

I frown and move to take the empty seat beside Travis, laughing lightly when I realize she's just given me a lunch hour detention slip. "You're kidding, right?"

"Purple hair, tattoos and body piercings aren't against

school policy, Mr Reid," she draws out, still jotting away at her desk. "The board wants students to feel free to *express themselves,* whatever that means, but while you're sitting in my classroom, you will wear the uniform without looking like you just spent a half hour in the bathroom with a grabby cheerleader."

The majority of the class bursts out laughing and I shake my head at her, discreetly sliding my eyes to the side to check Jordyn's reaction. She's not laughing like the rest, but I don't miss the way she keeps stealing glances at me when she thinks I'm not looking. I'm not the only one watching her, though, and when Noah slides his narrowed eyes from her to me, I swear I can practically *hear* the silent threat there.

Stay away from her.

But unfortunately for him, I'm not afraid of pretty boy douchebags who depend on their rich daddies to fight their battles for them, which is why I drop back in my seat and hold his eyes with a silent message of my own.

Make me.

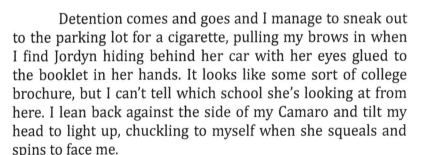

Detention comes and goes and I manage to sneak out to the parking lot for a cigarette, pulling my brows in when I find Jordyn hiding behind her car with her eyes glued to the booklet in her hands. It looks like some sort of college brochure, but I can't tell which school she's looking at from here. I lean back against the side of my Camaro and tilt my head to light up, chuckling to myself when she squeals and spins to face me.

This girl is so fucking jumpy.

She quickly hides the booklet behind her back like she's been caught doing something she shouldn't, only releasing the breath she was holding when she realizes I'm alone. "Jesus, you scared me."

"Sorry."

She raises a brow at that, somehow knowing I'm not sorry at all. "What are you doing out here?"

"Smokin' a cigarette," I say simply, eyeing her curiously while I blow my smoke out to the side. "What are *you* doing out here?"

"Nothing," she mutters, discreetly tossing the booklet across to her passenger seat in an attempt to hide it from me, but I already saw it.

"Washington?" I ask, amused. "What, did you pull out a map and pick the furthest school you could find?"

"Can you mind your own business?" she bites out, but something tells me that's not a rhetorical question – she's actually *asking* me if I can manage to keep my mouth shut about whatever it is I'm seeing here. "Please?" she adds, softer this time.

My brows dip and I run my tongue bar over my teeth, hiding a grin when her eyes drop to follow the sound.

"Fine." I nod, pushing myself off my car to level with her. "I'll keep your little college secret, but now you have to do something for me."

"And what's that?"

"Kiss me."

"*What?*" she chokes out. "Why?"

"*Why?*" I echo, laughing lightly when I realize she's actually expecting an answer to that. "Maybe I like you."

"Or *maybe* you just wanna fuck a princess," she fires back, crossing her arms over her chest with her head cocked to the side.

I smirk at that, knowing she's fishing but giving her nothing. If she wants to know if I'm the one who left her that birthday card on her car last night, she's gonna have to come right out and ask me.

"You say that like it's a bad thing," I tease, not missing the way she stares at my mouth while I step closer to her, only stopping when our bodies are almost touching. "And to answer your question.. yeah, it's gonna feel fucking amazing when it touches your clit."

Her jaw drops and she looks around to check no one's listening, her cheeks glowing the cutest fucking shade of pink I've ever seen. "I.. I wasn't thinking that."

"But you are now."

She swallows and cuts her eyes back to mine, but instead of walking away like I expected her to, she shocks the shit out of me and wraps her hand around the back of my neck, yanking me down to her until our faces are level. My brows jump and I rest my hands on the hood of the car either side of her head, silently waiting for whatever she'll do next. Her pastel blue eyes shine with a new found confidence and she smirks – fucking *smirks* at me – then she brushes her thumb over the corner of my mouth and pinches the cut there, forcing a pained groan from my throat while she pulls me in further.

"You think you're so hot, don't you?" she whispers against my lips, clicking her tongue while she digs her sharp nail into the sore spot. "Think again, new boy."

Fucking tease.

She kisses me once and shoves my head back just as

quick, casually slipping away from me like she didn't just make my dick hard. She shakes her ass for good measure and I reach down to readjust it, sliding my tongue over the fresh blood coating my lip.

"Hey, Jordyn?"

"It's JJ," she grits out, stopping half way up the front steps to face me fully.

"You were wrong before."

"About what?"

"I don't want a princess," I tell her, shamelessly moving my eyes over her sexy little outfit. "That little devil inside you? I wanna play with her."

8

Jordyn

"You know Penelope's been calling you, right?"

I roll my eyes at that, not even bothering to look her way while I continue taking notes from the board.

"Yes, Sienna, I'm aware."

Her and Noah have been blowing up my phone for the last ten days, but I haven't answered or read any of the messages they've sent me. Honestly, I'm *this* close to blocking their numbers just to get a little peace and quiet.

"Will you at least talk to her?" Sienna whispers, leaning over the desk between us to catch my eyes. "She's sorry and she misses you, but she can't tell you that if you keep shutting her out like this."

Fucking hell, really?

It's not like I was expecting our mutual friends to take my side or anything – they all knew she was fucking him anyway so it wasn't exactly a surprise to them – but I didn't think they'd try to make *me* out to be the bad guy, to make me feel like *I'm* the one who needs to step up and fix it.

It fucking sucks.

The last bell rings and I drop my pen, thankful I don't have to answer her. I take my time packing my books up and head for the door, keeping my eyes forward and my head held high while I make my way to my locker.

Never show weakness.

My mother's words ring through my head and I keep walking, flexing my fingers around the strap of my purse when I connect eyes with Xander Reid in the hall.

I don't know what the hell came over me in the parking lot last week, but instead of torturing myself by dwelling on it, I've decided to ignore him.

Indefinitely.

The bastard smirks like he knows it and I look away, making a quick stop at my locker to drop my books off before heading outside to my car. Ignoring the stares and whispers pointed my way, I jump inside and start the ignition, resisting the urge to bang my head against the steering wheel while I drive away towards home.

I can't wait to go to college next fall.

I won't be doing what *I* want to do, but at least I'll be somewhere other than this suffocating town.

I pull up on my driveway a few minutes later and head inside, jumping out of my skin when I hear my name being called out from behind me.

"JJ."

"Mom," I say back, breathing a long sigh of relief when I realize she didn't bring the Miami man home with her.

Last time she did that I earned myself a bridesmaid's dress and a bratty younger stepsister.

"Did you miss me?"

I nod and wrap my arms around her waist, resting my head on her chest to inhale her familiar scent. Her body stiffens and she lifts her hands, awkwardly patting my back when I don't release her right away. Those stupid tears fill my eyes but I force them back, silently pleading myself not to cry in front of her.

She doesn't handle emotion well.

"Are you alright?" she asks, gently pushing me back by my shoulders to brush the creases from her dress.

"Yeah."

"Are you sure?" She frowns, bouncing her eyes between mine. "You look.. I don't know. Are you sad?"

I laugh lightly at that, surprised she cares.

But that's not fair.

My mother *does* care about me, just not in the way I want her to. She cares about my social status and my popularity and my weight, whether or not I get accepted to an Ivy League school, whether or not I marry into the family she picked out for me when I was nothing more than an idea.

As for me and the way I feel, though..

I'm pretty sure she couldn't care less.

As long as we're good looking, rich and respected, nothing else matters.

"JJ?"

"Are you staying for dinner?" I ask, nervously wringing my hands together while I lead the way to the kitchen.

"Maryanne's not working today but she left me a salad in the fridge. You can have half if you want."

"But it's Thursday."

"So?"

"So.. don't you always have dinner with Noah and his parents on Thursdays?"

I nod and chew my lip, hesitating a second before I decide to bite the bullet. "We broke up."

"You *what*?!" she screeches, making me cringe. "Why?"

I keep my mouth shut and grab two plates from the cabinet overhead, busying myself dishing the food out and grabbing two waters from the fridge.

"JJ," she sighs, clearly displeased with me and my silence. "Whatever you did wrong, you need to fix it and get him b–"

"Jesus, he cheated on me with Penelope, Mom," I cut in, dropping down at the island to stab a piece of chicken with my fork. "*I* broke up with *him*."

Her jaw ticks and she props her hands on her hips, her obvious embarrassment for me reddening her cheeks and the tip of her nose. "Does everyone know?"

"Yep."

She exhales an aggravated breath and takes the seat across from me, folding her hands on the counter like we're about to negotiate a business deal. "Look, honey, I know this is hard, trust me, I *know*, but I need you to find a way to move past this. Your entire future depends on it, sweetheart."

A bitter laugh leaves me and I drop my fork on my plate, leaning back in my seat with my arms crossed over my chest. "You're joking, right?"

"No, I'm not *joking*, and I don't appreciate your tone."

"Yeah, well I don't appreciate *you* telling me I need to stay with the guy who's been sleeping around on me just to fulfil *your* big plan. I have my own plans, Mom."

"What plans?"

"Washington," I blurt out, swallowing my fear when I catch the look on her face, but I don't stop talking. "I wanna move to Seattle to study photography."

"*Photography*?" she echoes, scrunching her nose as if the thought insults her. "Since when?"

"Since *always*!" I shout, struggling to calm my sudden temper. "If you paid even a little bit of attention to me and my life, maybe you'd know that."

"And if *you* paid even a little bit of attention to your boyfriend, maybe he wouldn't have to go looking for it elsewhere!"

My jaw drops and my eyes burn with tears, my throat burning with a mixture of disgust and shame. She opens her mouth to say something else but I'm already gone, snatching my purse from the counter to make a beeline for the entryway.

"JJ!" she barks. "Where do you think you're going?"

"Out."

"I'm not finished talking to y–"

I slam the heavy front door behind me and jog down the front steps, fumbling with my keys to unlock my car. I jump inside and speed off towards the beach, hitting the breaks just as quick when I realize pictures won't cut it today.

I need to vent.

Hit something.

I turn around and drive down to the gym on the other side of town, barely paying attention to my surroundings while I grab my duffel bag from the trunk and sling it over my shoulder. Still wearing my school uniform, I walk inside and swipe my membership card over the scanner, pushing the bar to let myself in. Kian's older sister spots me through the window in her office and walks out to greet me, her warm smile fading when she catches the look on my face.

"Back room's all yours, babe."

"Thanks," I mutter, cursing myself when I hear the pathetic crack in my voice. "Hey, Kelly? Can you, uh, not tell Kian about this? Or anyone?"

She nods and I walk away, ignoring the eyes of the members working out on the main floor while I head through to the private room reserved for boxers. It's dark and cold in here, the only light coming from the sun creeping through the tiny, rectangular windows across the top of the back wall. I drop my bag down in the corner and change into my gym clothes, quickly tying my hair up into a messy ponytail at the top of my head. I leave the lights off and plug my phone in to crank the music up, then I slide my gloves over my hands and fasten the velcro with my teeth.

And then I vent.

9

Xander

"Dude, pay attention," I scold, quickly snatching the bar from Kian's trembling hands when he looks like he's about to fucking choke himself with it. "What the hell are you looking at?"

"Nothing," he rasps, tipping his head back on the bench to look at me upside down. "The view's pretty good from down here, though."

I raise a brow and lift the bar back up to the rack, walking around him to grab my water bottle from the floor. I take a sip and he struggles to sit up, resting his elbows on his thighs to drop his head in his hands.

"You guys do this every single day?" he asks, wincing while he rubs his sore muscles. "It *hurts*."

I chuckle and toss him a drink, still amused by his hot pink boy shorts and matching headband. He turned up at the house just as me and Travis were leaving for his sister's gym, said he wanted us to take him home to change so he could tag along and *play with the big boys*, as he put it. I don't know the guy well, but I'm pretty sure the heaviest thing he's ever lifted is his thigh to shave his scrawny little chicken legs in the shower.

Travis finishes his set and sits up to wipe the sweat from his forehead with his t-shirt, smirking to himself when he catches Kian's eyes on his abs. Kian drags his bottom lip out through his teeth and I cock my head at him, bouncing my eyes between the two boys who can't seem to keep their eyes off each other.

"Are you two fucking?"

Travis chokes on his water and Kian blushes like a nun, telling me all I need to know.

Boy's no fucking nun, and it seems my cousin knows it.

"Dude, will you shut the fuck up?" Travis hisses, quickly looking around to check no one heard me.

"Sorry."

He glares and I smirk, frowning when he swallows and scrubs a hand over his mouth. "Xan, listen–"

"Don't do that."

"Do what?"

"Explain yourself to me like it's something that needs an explanation," I say simply, rolling my eyes when he stares at me like I've grown two heads. "I know what fucking is, Trav. I do it all the time."

"That's different."

"*Why* is it different?"

He sighs out a breath and looks at Kian, smiling a little bit when he catches the look on his face. It's relief, but it's not the type I would have expected. He's not relieved over my no fucks to give reaction to their secret relationship, he's relieved Travis didn't panic and go off on me for bringing unwanted attention to it.

"I need a shower," Travis says, hitting me with a quick look that says *keep your fucking mouth shut or die*, then he stands and tilts his head for Kian to follow.

Kian jumps up like his ass is on fire and I shake my head at them, deciding to hang back a while because I don't feel like hearing my cousin fuck his boyfriend against the bathroom wall. "How long should I wait?"

"Thirty minutes."

"Fifteen," Kian calls over his shoulder. "And that's only because it takes him ten minutes to prep m–"

Travis smacks the back of his head and Kian yelps, making me laugh. The two of them head for the changing rooms down the hall and I move for the fountain to refill my water bottle, doing a double take at the door in the corner when I catch sight of the girl working out through the rectangular window. Her face is shadowed in darkness and she's got her body turned away from me, but I know it's her.

Jordyn fucking James.

I hesitate for all of three seconds before I'm moving, quickly checking to make sure no one's looking before I slip through the door. *Teardrops* by Bring Me The Horizon blares from somewhere and I look around, grinning to myself when I spot her phone plugged into the speaker set up in the corner.

I knew she liked this type of music, saw that sneaky little smile on her face when that emo vampire song came on at her house that night.

Right before she saw me for the first time.

Right after she helped that mousy haired girl get away from Penelope and Sienna.

Jordyn's good.

Way too good for me, but I don't give a shit.

I want her so fucking bad.

I stick to the shadows and lean back against the wall behind her, enjoying the way her hot little body moves while she beats the shit out of the bag hanging from the ceiling like it did her wrong.

She looks mad.

Ready to kill someone.

Sexy as hell.

She's wearing a black and green pair of camo sweats and a black sports bra, showing off her toned stomach and those tiny little bones on her hips. Her skin is hot and covered in a light layer of sweat, her cute little baby hairs sticking to her forehead while she lays it all out there, barely stopping to breathe between punches before she starts up all over again. My hands twitch with the urge to touch her and I almost fucking do it, almost step forward and snatch her waist to scare the shit out of her just because I can, but then I look at her face and catch the thick tears falling over her cheeks.

Fuck, is she *crying*?

My brows crash in the center and my stomach drops, the increasing need to take her in my arms coming from a whole new place this time.

I don't like that look on her face.

It's even worse than those fake ass smiles she hands out like party favors.

I watch her for another few seconds while I try to decide between asking her what's wrong and leaving her be, but then the door swings open and I look that way, rolling my eyes when Noah Campbell walks inside like he owns the damn world.

Fucking cockblock.

Little Devil

10

Jordyn

My chest heaves with the exertion but I keep going, ignoring the way my lungs are screaming for air and my body screams for me to stop.

Ignoring *him*.

Wishing he'd fuck off and leave me alone so I can sort through my rampant emotions in peace.

My song suddenly cuts off and I hit the bag one more time, spinning to look at the asshole who just pulled the cord from my phone. Noah hits me with that stupid golden boy grin of his and I openly glare at him, lifting my forearm to wipe my hair from my face.

"How did you find me?"

"I saw your car in the parking lot on my way home."

"So you *followed* me in here?"

"You won't talk to me, JJ," he fires back, throwing his hands out in annoyance. "You avoid me at school, you don't answer your phone or text me back, and your stupid staff won't even let me through your fucking door. What the hell do you expect me to do?"

I don't give a shit what he *does*, but I don't tell him that.

He sighs and steps closer to me, eyeing the traitorous tears still leaking from my eyes. "What happened?"

"My mom," I choke out, glaring at the ceiling with my gloves on my waist while I fight to compose myself.

Stop crying.

I take a deep breath and force my body to comply, cutting my eyes back to Noah to find him staring at me and my form, but it's not out of want. He doesn't like it when I wear sweatpants to work out, says they make me look like a twelve year old boy.

"What do you want, Noah?" I ask, no longer in the mood to answer his question.

"I want you back."

I laugh lightly at that, lifting my gloves up to my mouth to work on the velcro with my teeth. "I told you it's done. *We* are done."

"But we don't have to be," he argues, gently taking my wrists to help me with them. "If you can just let this go, we can get through this. We can be us again."

I open my mouth to argue but he shakes his head, dropping my gloves to the floor before moving in to take my face in his hands.

"Come on, JJ," he says. "Let me make it up to you."

I remain still and he takes full advantage, slowly sliding his hands down to my waist to pull me into him. He kisses the corner of my mouth and I tense, squeezing my eyes shut to banish the disgust at myself for allowing him to touch me. The weak, broken hearted little girl inside me begs me to cling to the only boy I've ever known, but instead of ignoring her like I should, I wrap my hands around his neck and smash my mouth on his. He exhales a relieved breath and I bite his lip, digging my nails into his flesh to encourage him to move faster. He winces and removes my hands from his neck, sweetly linking our fingers together while he moves his mouth down to my jaw. I roll my eyes and grit my teeth, silently begging the ceiling for patience while he continues to tease me with his lips.

He's always been clueless when it comes to making me feel good, never noticed the way I used to fake moans and orgasms just to get him to finish faster, and it seems tonight's no exception.

I want him to *take* me, to *own* me the way I watched him owning my best friend through the window that night, but he won't do it. Instead he takes it slow, handling me like I'm a fragile, expensive object he's afraid he'll break if he's not careful.

He wraps his arms around my back and I cringe, fisting my hands by my shoulders while I prepare myself to let him have me the way he wants me.

Speak your words, Jordyn James.

He pecks my lips again and I turn my head away, bravely shoving him back with as much force as I can manage. "*No.*"

"What the fuck, JJ?"

"I don't want that!" I shout, angrily wiping my mouth with the back of my hand. "I want.."

"What?" he bites out. "What do you want from me?"

"I.." I trail off, shaking my head at myself because it doesn't matter what I want.

It *never* matters what I want.

"She wants you to fuck her like you hate her."

I jump and spin in a half circle, searching the shadows to find the source of *that* voice. I find the cocky bastard a second later, narrowing my eyes when I catch that stupid smirk on his face. He's wearing a black pair of gym shorts and a black t-shirt, casually leaning back against the wall with his arms crossed over his chest like he's not being a total creep right now.

"How long have you been standing there?"

"What the fuck are you talking about?" Noah asks at the same time, scrunching his nose from beside me with a mixture of anger and confusion.

"Hate sex, man," Xander explains, rudely choosing to answer Noah's question over mine. "Hot. Wild. *Rough*.."

Noah looks at me and I look away, awkwardly dipping my head to tuck some stray hairs behind my ears. "No, I don't.. that's not–"

Xander steps forward before I can finish and snatches my waist with both hands, making me squeal. He yanks me into him and shoves me back in his spot against the wall, roughly curling his fingers beneath the waistband of my sweats to lift me off my feet. His knuckles brush the skin of my bikini line and I squeal again, instinctively wrapping my hands around his neck and my legs around his waist to keep myself steady.

"What the hell are you doing?!" I screech, struggling to ignore the way his body feels pressed up against mine.

He might not look like the type of guy who works out

every day without fail, but I'd bet my mother's company he's got at least eight abs under that shirt.

Instead of answering me, he slides his hands over my stomach and out towards my hips, squeezing me and digging his fingertips into the flesh there. My breathing picks up and he looks up at me, clearly enjoying my reaction to him and his hands on my body.

This is the first time he's touched me like this, the first time he's touched me *ever*, and despite the legitimate fear rushing through me right now, I don't hate it as much as I'm pretending to.

I fight him to save face and he smirks like the devil himself, not even bothering to hide the way his hard cock rubs against my clit through our clothes. Without thinking too much into it, I scrape my manicured nails over the sides of his neck and he groans out a curse, but he doesn't stop me the way Noah did just now. I think he *likes* it, and that pleases me more than it should.

"When you become mine," he says, dipping his head to run his tongue bar over my bottom lip. "I'm gonna make you moan with this, then I'm gonna pin you down on your back and fuck this needy little pussy until you come all over my dick. *Twice.*"

Jesus Christ.

I whimper before I can stop it and he chuckles against my mouth, pulling back an inch to search my eyes.

"Hear that, pretty boy?" he asks, speaking to Noah but looking directly at me. "*That's* what she wants."

I stare at him in shock and he stares right back at me, cocking his head to the left when Noah's bitter voice rings out from behind him. "Fucking slut."

I wince without meaning to and Xander sets me down on my feet, turning around to toss Noah back against the side of the ring. My mouth hangs open and he snatches Noah's jaw, moving in to get in his face.

"The fuck did you just call her?"

"You heard me," he sneers, but I don't miss the clear flash of fear there.

"Listen here, you little pussy," he warns, barely moving when Noah tries to shove him back. "Say shit like that to her again and I'll break your fucking nose."

Noah tries to say something else but Xander shoves his head away, easily pushing his ass to the floor before stepping over him like it was nothing.

"You stupid freak," Noah bites out, standing up to brush the imaginary dirt from his shirt. "I'll have you arrested for that."

"For *what?*"

"You just *assaulted* me, you idiot."

"Did I?" Xander frowns, making a show of looking around to emphasise the lack of cameras in here, then he smirks at him. "Prove it."

Noah glares and I fight a grin, scrubbing a hand over my mouth to hide it when both boys cut their eyes to mine.

"You wanna ride, princess?"

"I brought my car." I raise a brow, knowing he already knows that considering he was watching us talk before.

"Not what I meant," he teases, slowly moving his eyes over my body while he backs up towards the door.

A blush creeps up my neck and I fold my arms over my

chest, feigning indifference despite the heat coursing through me. "In your dreams, new boy."

"Damn straight." He winks, and then he's gone.

I shake my head at him and grab my gloves from the floor, ignoring the eyes on me while I shove the rest of my stuff into my gym bag.

"JJ–"

"Go to hell, Noah."

He shuts his mouth and I head outside through the fire escape in the corner, feeling surprisingly better about myself than I have in weeks.

Little Devil

11

Jordyn

"How much sugar is in this?"

"Too much for Mommy Dearest to find out about," Kian jokes, dropping down on the sun bed beside me. "We'll just have one treat and then stick to vodka, yeah?"

I laugh lightly and knock his glass with mine, leaning back in my own seat to sip the multicolored cocktail he made me just now. The early afternoon sun beats down on my body and I drop my sunglasses over my eyes, using the makeshift shield to scan the crowd of half naked teenagers without being obvious.

Me and just about every other senior are spending our Saturday in Kian's huge back yard, taking full advantage of the infinity pool and the fully stocked bar he paid for with his daddies' credit card this weekend.

I'd planned to skip the party and stay at home, but Kian showed up at my house just after lunch and practically wrestled me out the door, ensuring me he'd punch anyone who looked at me twice.

He's a lying little bitch, but I don't call him out on it.

Even three weeks later, people still stare at me and whisper shit when they think I'm not looking, and it doesn't help that Penelope's currently sitting with Sienna and Noah in the hot tub by the pool. She hasn't spoken to me directly and I hope it stays that way, but I don't miss the guilty looks she keeps giving me, half smiling at me like she's expecting me to go over there and clear shit up between us.

I do no such thing.

Penelope's a good actress and an even better manipulator, and I want no part in whatever twisted game she's trying to play with me.

"Babe, will you do my back for me?" Kian asks, turning over to lie on his front.

I nod and set my drink down on the coffee table between us, taking his pineapple scented sun screen from the mini fridge to squeeze a bit onto my palm. I work it into his shoulders and down to the band of his neon yellow speedos, not missing the eyes on my hands while I do it. I smirk to myself and lift my glasses to peek at Travis, subtly holding the bottle up with a look that says *you want it, all you gotta do is come and take it*. He stays where he stands and I shake my head at him, frowning when I spot Xander standing beside him with a sneaky little knowing look on his face.

What is he..?

"Xan knows."

My eyes widen and I look at Kian, unable to hide my surprise. "*What?*"

"Shh," he laughs, leaning up on his elbows to bring his face closer to mine. "He caught me staring at Travis when we were at the gym last week and–"

"The gym?"

"Yeah, he was helping me lift weights, spotting me or some shit," he explains, waving that off like it's irrelevant. "Anyway, he asked us straight up if we were fucking and we didn't deny it, then Travis took me to the bathroom and fucked me with his ton–"

"Okay," I cut in, slapping a hand over his mouth to shut him up. "I don't need to hear that part."

He laughs again and I drop my hands to my lap, confused as to why he's acting so calm about this. We all know Kian's gay but Travis isn't out yet, and if he's forced out or caught out before he's ready, I'm worried he'll freak and break Kian's heart in the process.

"Ki, he could tell somebody."

"Yeah, I thought that, too, but he was weirdly fine about it." He shrugs. "He even told Travis to shut up when he tried to explain it away. He won't say anything."

My brows dip and I look at Xander, honest to god wondering if he's not as much of an asshole as I've made him out to be, but then I catch him moving his greedy little eyes over my body and change my mind.

He's still an asshole.

He fails to hide that stupid grin of his and I roll my eyes for good measure, dropping back in my seat to take another small sip of my drink. He's made his intentions perfectly clear, more than once, but I'm not interested, and even if I was, I could never go there.

He's too cocky.

Too forward.

Too.. *different.*

But damn, he makes it look good.

He's leaning back against the pool table on the patio wearing a black pair of swim shorts and a black flannel shirt, the buttons all the way undone to expose his hard chest and solid abs. The several pieces of ink scattered across his body are mostly random – some good and some not so good – but somehow he makes it look more hot than ridiculous.

Not hot, JJ.

Shit.

"Dude, you're cheating," Travis accuses, earning both mine and Kian's attention.

Xander chuckles and leans over to take his shot. "I'm not a cheater, Trav. I'm just better than you."

The black ball lands in the corner pocket and Travis scoffs, taking the triangular rack from beneath to reset the table. "JJ, come here and kick his punk ass so I can laugh at him for losing to a girl."

I laugh lightly and open my mouth to tell him I'm good here, but then I catch the surprise on Xander's face and snap it shut again.

"You're good at pool?"

"She's the fucking *boss* at pool," Kian answers for me, snatching my hand to pull me over to them. "There's a reason we call her queen, new boy, and it ain't got nothin' to do with that ass you won't stop staring at."

"*Kian.*"

"What?"

"Shut up," I whisper through my teeth, walking around

him to get to Travis.

He passes me the cue he was just using and takes out a quarter from the back pocket of his shorts, tipping his chin at me while he tosses it into the air. "Call it."

"Heads."

He catches the coin and flips it over, removing his hand to get a look at it. "You start, JJ."

I make my way around to the far end of the table and lean over to break the balls, immediately sinking two solids right off the bat. Travis and Kian both grin like idiots and I dip my head to hide mine, purposely ignoring the asshole opposite me while I move around to take my next shot.

I'm wearing a baby pink, strapless two piece to keep my tan lines to a minimum. My breasts are a little too big for my body, same goes for my ass and thighs, which is why my mother forces me to avoid sugar and carbs of any kind, but it seems Xander doesn't mind my flaws considering he can't take his eyes off them.

"Hey, Jordyn?"

My jaw ticks but I refrain from correcting him, knowing he'll just continue to call me that anyway. "What?"

"I dare you to play a game with me."

"Pool *is* a game, new boy," I say dryly, leaning over to pot the five ball.

"Yeah, well, this is more like a bet than a game."

"What's the bet?"

"If you win, I'll stop talking to you and leave you alone for the rest of the year."

My brows crash in the center and I look up, ignoring

the pang of hurt in my chest because it's misplaced and pathetic. "And if you win? What do you get?"

"*When* I win," he says smugly, leaning his elbows on the edge of the table to level with me. "You have to do everything I say for twenty four hours."

"Like a slave?"

"Like a date," he corrects me, laughing lightly when I slip up and miss my shot.

"Xan.." Travis warns from beside Kian, not so subtly shaking his head no.

"What?"

"What do you mean, *what*?" I hiss, quickly checking left and right to ensure no one else is listening to our conversation. "I'm not going on a date with you."

"Why not?"

"Because I don't like you."

He raises a brow at that, somehow knowing I'm a liar. "You wanna play or not?

"A date doesn't last twenty four hours."

"Twelve, then."

"Two."

"Six."

"What the hell are we gonna do for six hours?"

A slow, dirty little smirk spreads across his face and I drop my jaw, struggling to hide the heat creeping up my neck and over my cheeks.

"You're disgusting."

"Is that a yes?"

"Jesus, just–" I stop myself from going off on him and take a breath, lowering my voice while I back away to give him room. "Just take your damn shot."

He grabs his cue and leans over to do as he's told, easily sinking three balls without issue. "Your boyfriend's watching us, you know?"

I roll my eyes and fold my arms over my chest, avoiding Noah's glare on the side of my face while I lean my ass back against the table. "He's not my boyfriend anymore."

"Does *he* know that?" he throws back, pausing to look up at me when I don't answer. "I can help you make him jealous if you want."

"I don't need to make him jealous."

"I know." He grins, straightening up to crowd my space. "I just wanted to kiss you again."

Kian chokes on his cocktail and I grind my teeth, ignoring the three of them while I turn my attention back to the game. We're neck and neck with five balls left on the table and it's my turn to shoot. I could be wrong, but I swear he missed that last shot on purpose.

He's offering me an out.

A way to say no if I want to.

I swallow my sudden nerves and bend over to pot my last two solids, looking at Xander over my shoulder when I feel his heat at my back. "Do you mind?"

He lifts his hands up in mock surrender and backs up a couple steps, but he doesn't move from behind me. I let out an aggravated breath and force myself to pay attention, pretending I don't feel the odd sense of excitement running

Little Devil

through me with his eyes on my ass.

One more shot and it's over.

I line it up and keep my eyes on the eight ball, hesitating a little longer than necessary before I pull my arm back to take the shot. It only takes me a half a second to realize my mistake, and as soon as the white hits the black, it rebounds off the edge of the side pocket and I miss.

Shit.

Travis and Kian both stare at me in disbelief and Xander smirks to himself, casually pressing his chest to my back to speak in my ear. "I'll pick you up at eight."

"Wh– *tonight?*" I stammer, spinning to face him fully. "Why can't we do it next weekend?"

"Because I want you now."

I gape at him and he sinks the last three balls one after the other, winking at me while he sets his cue down and walks off towards the bar. My heart leaps up into my throat and I lift my hand to cover it, swallowing the unease there while I tip my head back to look at the sky.

What the fuck did I just do?

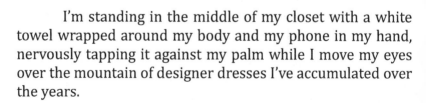

I'm standing in the middle of my closet with a white towel wrapped around my body and my phone in my hand, nervously tapping it against my palm while I move my eyes over the mountain of designer dresses I've accumulated over the years.

He didn't tell me where we're going or what we're

doing or what to wear, and now I'm officially freaking out over my *date* like a thirteen year old girl.

I consider calling Travis to get him to give me Xander's number but decide against it, knowing that's stupid, then I consider calling to tell him I'm not going but decide against that, too.

This is pathetic.

Taking a long breath in an attempt to rebuild my sinking self-esteem, I grab the black dress I've had my eye on since I came in here and snatch a strappy pair of red bottoms to match, then I take my hair straightener from the bottom drawer and walk out to my bedroom, dropping down at my dressing table to get to work.

Little Devil

12

Xander

"You're really gonna go through with this?" Travis asks, sitting back on the couch in the pool house with a beer in his hands and his eyes on me.

"Go through with what?"

"Forcing JJ to go on a date with you."

"I'm not *forcing* her to do shit," I argue, pulling out a black t-shirt from my closet to throw it on over my head. "She could've said no."

He rolls his eyes and I check my hair in the mirror, secretly excited for the night I have planned for her.

I've never been on a date before.

I'm used to picking up random girls at parties and going from there, but I've never gotten the chance to really earn it like I get to do with Jordyn.

It's fucking thrilling.

I say goodbye to Bear and pocket my phone and wallet, bumping Travis' fist on my way to the door.

"Don't you dare fuck her, Xan."

"Is that a dare?" I joke, laughing lightly when he bangs his head back against the couch and covers his eyes with his forearm.

Such a fuckin' drama queen.

I get to Jordyn's house a couple minutes before eight and pull up on the driveway, jumping out of my car to walk up to the front door. I'm just about to knock, but then the door swings open and Jordyn appears with only one shoe on and her purse clutched under her arm, breathing heavily like she just ran all the way down here to get the door for me.

"Oh, shit, you look ho–"

"Are you out of your mind?" she hisses, angrily walking me back with a hand on my chest. "You were just gonna knock on my front door and say *hey, Maryanne, I'm here to pick up Jordyn for our date?*"

"What's wrong with that?"

She glares and holds on to my shoulder while she bends over to wrestle her other shoe on, then she straightens up and takes her phone out to set the timer for six hours. "Let's just get this over with."

I roll my lips and she moves her pretty blue eyes over my form, awkwardly tugging on the hem of her dress while I follow her down to my car to open the passenger side door for her.

She's wearing a little black dress similar to the first one she was wearing at her birthday party that night. It's skin tight with a low neck line, sitting mid thigh with two thin spaghetti straps meeting at the back of her neck. Her skin is darker than usual and practically glowing thanks to her time in the sun at Kian's house today, her shiny blonde hair straightened over her shoulders in a way that makes it look even longer if that's possible.

She's so fucking beautiful.

And mean.

And a little hesitant, I think.

"Are you getting in?"

She clears her throat and climbs inside, avoiding my eyes while she pulls her seatbelt on over her chest. I shut the door for her and round the front of the car, jumping in beside her to start the ignition.

"What's wrong, princess?"

"Nothing," she mutters, sighing when I lean back and raise a brow at her, refusing to move until she speaks up about whatever it is that's bothering her. "It's just.. do you want me to go change into something more.. I don't know, *less*? Or *more*? You didn't tell me what to wear and now I feel a little overdressed."

"Do *you* wanna change?"

"I don't–"

I cock my head and she shuts her mouth, somehow reading my mind without me having to say it.

Speak your words, Jordyn James.

"Uh, no," she admits, her cheeks heating the way I know they do when she's embarrassed. "I like this one."

"Then no, I don't want you to change," I say simply, pulling away to drive towards the gate at the end of her driveway. "You're perfect just the way you are, Jordyn. Don't let any fucker tell you different."

She says nothing and I look her way, slowing to a stop when I catch her staring at me with her mouth parted. I lean over to crowd her space and she swallows what looks like fear, but she doesn't pull away from me.

"Do you trust me?" I ask, lifting my hand to brush my thumb over her bottom lip.

She narrows her eyes and I laugh before I can stop it, lightly kissing the tip of her nose before I pull back to put the car in first. I hit the gas and she squeals, quickly grabbing on to the door handle to brace herself.

"What the hell are you doing?!"

"Driving," I chuckle, easily maneuvering my way through the streets the same way I've been doing since I was tall enough to reach the pedals.

She mutters something I don't catch and squeezes her eyes shut at every turn, only releasing the breath she's been holding when I hit the highway, probably because she can't feel how fast I'm going on a straight road like this. She looks ready to scream at me, or hit me, or both, but of course she doesn't do either of those things.

"You're taking me to the city?" she asks, pulling her sun visor down to reapply the lip gloss I must have ruined when I touched it just now.

"Is that okay?"

Her brows dip but she nods, visibly relaxing like she's relieved she won't have to worry about being seen with me in Lakewood where everybody knows her. I'm not offended, though, partly because her animosity towards me makes me laugh but mostly because something tells me she'll be more herself away from that stupid town she rules with a fake personality and a smile to match.

A little while later, I pull up in the parking lot by the beach and kill the ignition, climbing out and rounding the car to open her door. She looks up at me and I hold my hand out for her, purposely making a show of placing hers in mine when she continues to stare at me like I've grown two heads.

"What are y–"

"You need to relax," I tell her, pulling her out to lead her over to the strip of well lit restaurants and bars across the street. "You're makin' me nervous."

"*You* get nervous?" she asks, clearly not buying it. "I call bullshit."

"Did you just say *bullshit*?"

"I can say *bullshit* if I want."

I smirk at her over my shoulder and keep hold of her hand, guiding her in front of me by her waist while we make our way through the busy crowd. We get to the pizza place I found out here a couple weeks ago and I push the door open over her head, amused by the clear look of confusion on her face while I follow her inside.

"You know what you want?"

"Uh, no," she says, standing up on her tip toes to look at the menu on the counter. "I've never had pizza before."

"You've never had *pizza*?" I echo, pulling my head back in surprise. "How is that even possible?"

She shrugs and drops her eyes, tucking her hair behind her ears while she stares at the checkered floor like she's fascinated by it. My brows dip and I chew the inside of my cheek, gently lifting her chin until her eyes hit mine. I haven't known her long, but I've never seen her eat anything more than a few bites of lettuce in the cafeteria at school, and I'm betting that has less to do with her and more to do with that bitch of a mother I've heard so much about. Her and the asshole ex-boyfriend who made her change her clothes like he had the right.

"Can you not do that?" she asks, pulling her face from my hand. "I don't need you to feel sorry for me."

"I don't feel sorry for you," I say honestly, walking her along to the front of the line. "I feel sorry for them."

She stares at me and I turn to the cute girl behind the counter wearing a black and red uniform and a snap back to match. She takes our order and nods along, reaching over to grab a couple paper cups from the stack on her left while she taps away on her screen.

"Pineapple or no pineapple?"

I look at Jordyn and she frowns, bouncing her eyes from me to the pizza girl and then back to me again. "I don't understand the question."

"Pineapple doesn't belong on pizza, princess," I inform her, taking my wallet out to toss a fifty down on the counter. "It's a thing."

"Why?"

"It just is."

"I want the pineapple," she insists, crossing her arms over her chest like she thinks I'm about to fight her on it.

I give her what she wants and we take our drinks, waiting just a few minutes before I take the pizza box from the guy at the end of the counter. I guide Jordyn to the exit and she frowns again, looking at me over her shoulder.

"We're not eating in here?"

I shake my head and hold the door open for her with my forearm, shamelessly moving my eyes over her body while she passes me.

"Fuck me, you're hot."

The group of good looking guys behind her all voice their agreement and she drops her jaw, gaping at me with a hilarious look of outrage on her face.

I like making her do that.

Without thinking too much into it, I wrap my arm around her back and pull her into me, molding her to my chest while I lean over to tease her lips with mine.

I'd kill for her to let me put a bar through that hot little tongue of hers, to have her look up at me from her knees while she licks the length of my cock with it.

Goddamn.

I release her before I do something that'll get me slapped and she falls in line beside me, shocked into silence, it seems, but I don't miss the tiny little smile she's failing to hide. We get back to my car and I set the food down on the hood, taking her waist to lift her up and place her down next to it. I jump up to sit beside her and flip the box open, passing her a slice before grabbing one for myself. I pick the pineapple off and she shakes her head at me, eating quietly for a minute before she tips her chin at the ocean right in front of us.

"You like the water?"

"I'm from California, remember?"

"Can you surf?"

"No," I admit, laughing to myself at the memory of Nik trying to teach me when we were little.

I ended up in the hospital with a broken ankle and my parents lost their shit, yelled at Nik for getting me hurt and grounded him for two weeks.

It was hilarious.

"Can you?"

"Can I what?"

"Surf," I draw out, raising a brow when I realize she's staring at me again.

She shakes her head no and opens her mouth to speak, but then she changes her mind and looks away.

"Say it."

She rolls her eyes and grabs another slice of pizza, hesitating a minute before she decides to do as she's told. "You're just.. not what I expected, I guess."

"How's that?"

"I don't know." She shrugs, pausing to take a sip of her drink. "I mean, when I first saw you I thought you looked like a quiet loner boy, but then you opened your mouth and turned into this cocky, big headed player with no chill."

I chuckle at that, turning my head to tip my chin at the guy walking along the street with a black hood pulled over his head and his hands in his pockets. "What's the first thing that comes to mind when you look at him?"

"I.." she trails off, confused by the change of subject. "I don't kno–"

"Don't think. First thing, princess."

"Cross the street. He'll stab me."

"Alright." I nod, expecting that. "What if I told you his grandmother's dying in a nursing home not far from here, and he dresses like that when he goes to see her because he knows she likes it?"

A tiny grin betrays her and she looks away, side eyeing him from beneath her lashes. "You don't know that."

"Just like you don't know he'll stab you," I argue, lightly bumping her elbow with mine. "Ever heard of *don't judge a book by its cover*?"

"Ever heard of Jack the Ripper?"

I bark out a laugh and she grins for real this time, looking awfully proud of herself while she leans over to steal a small piece of pineapple from the lid of the box between us. The move brings her closer to me and I lift her chin with my forefinger, dropping my eyes to her mouth to watch her eat it.

"You should change the way you look at people."

"Isn't that dangerous?"

"Sometimes," I admit, dipping my head to brush my nose against hers. "But sometimes danger can be fun."

She pulls in a long breath of air and lets it out slowly, mindlessly sliding her tongue over her bottom lip while she stares at mine.

"Hey, Jordyn?"

"What, Xan?" she whispers, choosing this moment to use my name for the first time since I met her.

"I dare you to swim with me."

Little Devil

13

Jordyn

He must be out of his mind.

"Are you out of your mind?" I voice my thoughts, momentarily stunned by his stupidity. "Why the hell would I do that?"

"Because I dare you," he says, plain and simple as if it's just that easy for him.

I blink and he slides off the hood of his car, pulling his t-shirt over his head to toss it onto the back seat.

"It's really cold in there," I inform him, gesturing to the water to distract myself from his abs.

"Don't be a pussy."

"I am not a pussy."

"Prove it," he challenges, looking right at me while he pops the button on his jeans. "Quit acting like a good girl for once in your life and make a fucking mess."

"I'm not *acting*."

"You sure?"

I sigh and swallow the last of my pizza, wiping my hands with a napkin before I decide to stand up and do as he says. I walk over to him and bend over to remove my shoes, placing them down into the footwell beside his, then I pull my dress over my head and toss it onto the back seat next to his clothes. I'm left in a black lacy thong with a strapless bra to match and he's wearing nothing but his boxers, hard and ripped and sexy as hell.

"I'm not taking my underwear off."

"That's okay," he says quietly, reaching out to run his thumb over the edge of my thong at my bikini line. "I can just pull this to the side."

My jaw hangs wide open and he lifts his eyes to my mouth, trapping his bottom lip between his teeth to cover his laughter.

"Can you stop doing that?"

"Doing what?" he asks innocently, attempting to keep a straight face but failing.

"Staring at my tongue like you wanna suck on it."

He makes a noise that sounds like a cross between a choke and a groan, leaning over me to rest his forehead on mine. "You said that on purpose, didn't you?"

"Maybe," I tease, backing away from him to make my way down to the water.

He follows me and I take a breath to ready myself, toeing the shoreline for a second to test the temperature, but then the bastard wraps his arm around my waist from behind and lifts me off my feet.

"Xan!" I squeal, frantically kicking my legs out while he walks me forward and drags me into the ocean.

"Don't you know it's better to just dive right in?" he jokes, laughing at me when I try to wiggle myself free. "I thought you said you *weren't* a pussy."

"Oh my god, you're such an asshole!"

"You're sexy when you curse," he teases, leaning over me to nip my earlobe.

I squeal again and elbow his ribs, finally gaining enough leeway to spin around to face him. The water's up to my collarbone now and it's fucking freezing, but I can't help the big ass grin splitting my lips. He grins back and slides his hands over my waist, pulling me into him to wrap my legs around his hips. The warmth of his body feels good against mine and I rest my forearms on his shoulders, taking the opportunity to study every inch of his face while he's this close to me.

He's hot, but it's more than that.

I like his energy and the way he talks, the way he does whatever the hell he wants without worrying what other people might think of him.

He doesn't care.

He simply does not give a shit, and that excites me more than it should.

I wish I could be like him.

"What's your deal with all the dares?" I ask, running my fingers through his stupid purple hair to emphasise my question.

"Me and my older brother started this game when we were little," he explains, slowly running his hands over my outer thighs. "Sort of like a running joke. I'd dare him to do some stupid shit and he'd do the same to me, and whoever said no first would lose the game."

"Who lost?"

"Well, technically, no one did. It's still going on."

"For how long?"

"Thirteen years, I think."

My mouth parts but I close it just as quickly, frowning to myself while I try to sort through what Travis has told me about his family over the years. It's not much – he never even mentioned Xander to me before he moved here – but I don't remember him telling me anything about another cousin on his mother's side.

"Where's your brother?"

"He was killed in a bar fight when I was fifteen."

"Oh," I say sadly, gently sliding my thumb over the water running down his temple. "What was he like?"

His brows jump and I wince, inwardly cursing myself for asking such a stupid question. Most people would say they're sorry for his loss and move on to something else, which is obviously what I should have done.

"I'm sorry," I rush to explain. "I didn't mean t–"

"No, it's okay," he cuts in, staring at me for a long minute before he shakes his head to snap himself out of it. "He was.. wild and hilarious and moody and competitive, probably would've tried to steal you from me in under five seconds if he were here."

I raise a brow at that. "I'm not yours to steal from."

"Yet," he adds, laughing lightly when I flick a little

water at his face.

He flicks some right back and I turn my head away, not considering the consequences of my actions before I lift myself up to dunk his head under the surface. He comes back up to spit the water out of his mouth and I back away from him, raising my hands in mock surrender when I catch the look on his face.

"Xan.."

"Jordyn.."

"Don't you dar–"

He rushes me and I scream, laughing my ass off when he locks his arms around me to pull me under. I jump back up to wipe the hair from my face and splash him again, running away from him with a squeal when he starts to chase me. We mess around in the water for I don't know how long, and even though my hair is a mess and my make up is gone, this is the most fun I've had in months – probably years, if I'm being real.

I wish I brought my camera with me.

"Princess."

"What, new boy?"

"Are you done?"

"Yeah," I rasp, propping my hands on my waist to catch my breath.

He chuckles and follows me out to walk up to the tiny shower at the top of the beach. The water pressure sucks and does nothing to rinse the salt from my hair, but at least I won't be walking around with dried lumps of sand wedged between my toes.

"Hang on, I think I've got a clean towel in my gym bag," he tells me, quickly heading back to the car to grab it.

He hands it to me and I smile at him, leaning over to the side to dry my hair with it. "What now, Xander Reid?"

He shrugs and looks around, tipping his chin at the lit up nightclub across the street. "You wanna dance?"

"Xan, this is a bad idea," I hiss, awkwardly tugging my dress down over my thighs while he pulls me along by my hand. "I'm telling you they're not gonna let us in. Look at the state of my hair."

"It's sexy."

"It's *wet*."

He laughs at me and keeps walking, highly amused by me and my mini temper tantrum.

We put our clothes back on behind the car just now and I managed to fix my make up in the side mirror, but neither of us are wearing any underwear and I'm pretty sure everyone can see my ass through this dress.

"Xan–"

"Baby, chill," he says, pulling me in to back me up against the wall next to a fancy looking sushi restaurant. "You look hot, okay? *Really* fucking hot."

I remove the glare from my face and take a breath, secretly liking the way he calls me *baby*.

"Are you good?" he asks, speaking over my lips. "Or do you need to stay out here and listen to me tell you how bad I wanna fuck you up against this wall right now?"

Jesus Christ, he's too much.

Unable to form a verbal response to that, I shake my head and he winks at me, casually linking his fingers with mine while he walks me along towards the club we're about to try and con our way into. We get to the entrance and I stand up a little taller, doing my best to act casual and *chill* like he told me to. The bouncer frowns at me and I die a little on the inside, terrified I'm about to spend the night in jail, but then Xander pays the entry fee and passes him two driver's licenses. The bouncer takes them and looks between us for what feels like forever, passing them back with a nod and waving us in without so much as a second glance. My brows crash in the center and I look at Xander, snatching the fake cards from his hands to get a look at them. One of them is obviously his, but *my* picture is on the other one with a name that's not mine and a birthday that makes me twenty two.

"Damn it, you could have told me," I whisper yell, angrily shoving the cards at his chest when I catch the look on his face.

He keeps laughing at me and it's pissing me off.

"When did you even get that?"

"Today."

"*Today*," I echo, knowing he'd have only had about three hours to get it done, if that. "How?"

"I know a guy," he says vaguely, pulling me along through the dimly lit hallway to get to the main part of the club.

Neon pink strobe lights pulse throughout the room in time with the beat of the deafening music and there's a lit bar set up along the left wall, the right wall lined with black tables and chairs while the middle of the room serves as a huge dance floor.

I've never been in a place like this before.

I'm used to mansions and yacht parties and charity functions in ballrooms filled with expensive things to match the expensive people within.

Xander leads me over to the bar and takes out a wad of cash from his wallet, pulling me into him to shout in my ear. "You want a shot?"

I hesitate but nod, suddenly craving something to take the edge off. He orders us two each and knocks his glass against mine, eyeing me while I tip my head back to swallow it down. The vodka burns my throat and I wince at the aftertaste, setting my glass down on the bar to neck the other one just as quick.

"You alright, princess?" he chuckles, somehow sensing my inexperience and naivety.

"I need to go to the bathroom."

He nods and looks around, tipping his chin at the dark corner on the other side of the room. "You want me to go with you?"

I shake my head and back away from him to go by myself, somehow managing to snake my way through the crowd of dancers and drunk people without getting kidnapped or trampled on. I push the bathroom door open and choose a stall, scrunching my nose at the tampon slash condom machine in the corner.

This place is so weird.

I wash my hands once I'm done and check myself in the long, horizontal mirror above the counter, not exactly hating the look of the girl staring back at me.

She doesn't look like me.

I like that about her.

I walk out of the bathroom and make my way through the crowd again, ignoring the slurred pick up lines thrown my way while I scan the bar to look for Xander. I spot him sitting exactly where I left him and head that way, but then a pretty brunette girl grabs a hold of my hand and starts dancing with me. She's wearing a white mini dress and a veil to match, clearly drunk enough to assume she knows me, but she also seems harmless, which is why I decide it's safe to humor the bride to be for a minute. We dance together for the rest of the song and she stumbles into my arms a few times, making me laugh. After my fourth time setting her back on her feet, she wanders back over to her friends and I continue to dance on my own, lifting my arms over my head while I roll my hips to the beat of the music. *Rumors* by Neffex blares through my ears and I look up, biting my lip to hide the smile on my face when I catch Xander watching me from across the room. He's leaning back in his seat with his back to the bar and his legs spread out wide, ignoring the smoking hot girl pawing at his arm while he moves his eyes over my form.

Jealousy, you vile little bitch.

I expect the cocky bastard to sit on his ass and wait for me to come to him, but he doesn't do that. Instead he swallows the last of his drink and passes her the empty glass, never once taking his eyes off my body while he stands up and walks over to me.

"That was mean," I tell him, still rolling my hips out to the beat of the music surrounding us.

"I don't care," he teases, sliding his hands over my ribs to pull me into him. "And neither do you."

I smirk to myself and lower my arms to wrap them around his neck, enjoying the way his hard body feels against my soft one. He grinds on me and I move with him hit for hit, bravely running my hands through his messy hair to pull his face down to mine.

Noah never danced with me like this.

He never danced with me *period*, never took me out for pizza and sat me down on the hood of his car by the beach, never made me laugh until my insides hurt or looked at me like I'm the hottest girl he's ever seen.

Xander doesn't have that problem.

The fact that he's not even *trying* to hide his hunger for me turns me on more than I care to admit, and I'm pretty sure I'm in way over my head here.

I shouldn't be doing this with him.

He's bad and I'm good – or at least that's what I'm supposed to be – but right now, I don't give a fuck.

He slides his hands down to my ass and I moan before I can stop it, tightening my grip on his hair while I drop my eyes to his mouth. My heart races and I run my tongue over my lips, wanting it more than my next breath but too chicken to take it.

"Fuck, baby," he rasps, sounding just as worked up as I am. "You want me to kiss you, don't you?"

I nod without thinking and he smashes his mouth on mine, eagerly digging his fingers into my ass to pull me in further. I can't get close enough and it seems he feels the same way, because then I'm in the air and he's moving us towards the wall, pushing me up against it to trap my body with his. I bite his lip and he groans into my mouth, pulling my jaw down with his free hand to open me up for him. His piercing slides across my tongue and I moan again, thankful it's too loud in here for anyone but him to hear the noises I'm making.

"Xan."

"What, baby?"

"Take me home."

He freezes at that, pulling back an inch to bounce his eyes between mine. "What?"

"Take me home," I repeat, slower this time. "Now."

He stares at me for a solid ten seconds and I almost think he's about to tell me no, but then he grins like the devil he is and slides his thumb over his bottom lip, taking my hand to pull me out towards the exit. We get outside and I turn right to head to the parking lot, freezing when he pulls me back and takes me over to the first yellow cab parked up on the side of the road.

"What about your car?"

"I'll get it tomorrow."

He opens the back door for me and ushers me inside, giving the driver my address while he slides in to sit beside me. I frown at the worn fabric beneath my ass and run my finger over the hole next to my bare thigh, squealing when Xander snatches my waist and pulls me over to set me down on his lap.

"What the hell are you doing?" I hiss, but he just smirks and spreads my thighs apart so that I'm straddling him.

"Hey," the driver says, craning his neck from the front seat to get a look at us. "Put her back–"

Xander passes him a few fifty dollar bills and he shuts his mouth, muttering something about *horny fucking kids* while he pockets the cash and continues driving. I scrunch my nose at him and Xander pulls my eyes back to his, moving in to kiss the crook of my neck.

"Ignore him, baby. He's just jealous."

"Jealous of what?"

"The fact that you're mine and not his," he says, moving his hands down to squeeze my ass over my dress.

My pussy throbs and I clench my thighs around him, digging my nails into his shoulders to relieve some of the pressure. "I told you I'm not yours."

"*Yet*," he repeats, gently sucking on the flesh beneath my ear. "But you will be. Really fuckin' soon."

I pretend he didn't say that and run my hands over his chest, pausing to study the silver cross hanging around his neck. It's clearly fake considering there's barely any weight to it, probably one of those things you can pick up at the gift shop on the beach for a few dollars, if that, but the way he wears it every day without fail makes me think it's worth more to him than any diamond. He allows me to do my thing and I move my hands over his shoulders, then up to his face to brush my thumbs over the two circular piercings on either side of his nose.

"Did they hurt?" I ask, pulling his bottom lip down to get a look at the little bar in his tongue.

"Not as much as the other one."

My hand freezes on his mouth and I cut my eyes back to his. "Where's the other one?"

His smirk returns at the eagerness in my tone and he takes my wrist, slowly moving my hand over his abs and down to the waistband of his jeans. I swallow my fear and curl my fingers beneath the denim, my cheeks heating when I feel the two metal balls right there on the tip of his cock. I look down and run my thumb over the small space between them, clearing my throat when I realize how hard he is between my legs.

"This was a dare, too?" I guess, and he nods, breathing heavily against my forehead.

"My friend Justin made me do it after I dared him to tag his own house on Halloween last year. He's an asshole."

"A bigger asshole than you, you mean?"

He pinches my ass and I laugh at him, pulling his waistband out a little more to get a better look at this new piercing. I run two fingers over the tip and slowly swirl them around, fascinated and turned on by the thought of what it would feel like inside me.

"Jordyn," he warns, tangling his fingers in my hair to pull my mouth back to his. "If you keep playing with my dick like that, I'm gonna pull this dress up over your ass and fuck you right here in front of him."

My eyes widen and I stop what I'm doing, discreetly glancing at the driver over my shoulder before looking back at Xander.

Shit.

"You like that?" he asks, and I quickly shake my head to deny it, but he already caught me. "Dirty little devil," he whispers, tightening his grip on my ass to pull me down on him. "Rub your pussy on my dick and make yourself come. I wanna watch you."

I must have lost my mind someplace between my house and this cab, because instead of telling him no like I should, I whimper and wrap my hands around his neck, unable to stop the way my hips roll out to chase the friction he's offering. I kiss him like he's mine and he shoves his tongue into my mouth, leaning back even further to grind his hips up against me. He's driving me wild and it's right fucking *there*, but it's just out of reach and I can't get a good enough hold on it.

"Baby," he pleads. "Let me touch your pussy."

I nod a little faster than necessary and he brushes his thumb over my clit, groaning out a curse when he feels how wet I am for him. I slap a hand over his mouth and whip my head over my shoulder, wincing a little bit when I catch the driver's eyes in the rear view. His face reddens and he clears his throat, averting his eyes while he shifts around in his seat. Xander chuckles against my hand and I cut my eyes back to his, jolting against him when he increases the pressure on my clit.

"*Fuck*," I mouth, pulling his head back by his hair to kiss him again. "I need more, Xan."

He licks my tongue and twists the hand between my legs, sliding a single finger inside me to give me what I asked for. I dig my nails into his scalp and bite his lips, shamelessly rolling my hips on his lap to chase the high. His thumb finds my clit again and my mouth parts, my eyes rolling back in their sockets while I fall apart from the inside out. I fall down on his chest and rest my forehead against his, shaking my head at him when I catch the stupid grin on his face.

"What the hell are you doing to me, new boy?"

"I don't know but I like it."

I roll my eyes at that, dipping my head to hide my own grin because *yeah, I think I like it, too.*

14

Xander

Her bedroom door crashes against the wall and she stumbles in my arms, clinging to the back of my neck to keep herself steady. She tears at my clothes like they offend her and fists the hem of my t-shirt, pulling it up over my head to toss it on the floor. I take her waist and back her up towards the bed, shoving her down on her back to move my eyes over her hot little body. Her legs part without instruction and I barely contain my groan, kneeling up on the edge of the bed between her thighs to run my hand over my cock through my jeans.

She keeps surprising me and I like it.

I like it a fucking lot.

She chews her lip like she's considering something and then reaches over to turn the bedside lamp off, frowning at me when I snatch her wrist to stop her.

"What?"

"I wanna see you," I tell her, pushing her back to pop

the button on my jeans. "All of you."

She swallows and leans up on her elbows, watching me curiously while I pull my zipper down to give my dick a little breathing room. I've been hard since the second she wrapped her legs around me in the water earlier tonight, and just the sight of her spread out beneath me like this isn't helping the state of my sanity.

I push her dress up to her ribs and pull it over her head, tossing it down onto the baby pink rug on the floor next to my shirt. Her bedroom is immaculate and huge, at least four times the size of my room back at my parents' house. She's got one of those four poster beds made up with white sheets and pink throw pillows, a white corner couch on the other side of the room with a coffee table and three expensive looking paintings hanging on the wall above it, and a white vanity behind me with a fresh bunch of pink flowers on top.

"Nice apartment, princess," I joke, leaning over her to tease her nipple with my thumb.

"Shut up," she chuckles, wrapping her hand around the back of my neck to pull my mouth back to hers. "I don't even like this room. This is just what my interior designer *thinks* I should like."

"Your *interior designer*," I echo, sliding my tongue bar over her lip. "Poor little rich girl."

"Says the boy with the Camaro," she throws back, squealing when I pinch her nipple between my fingers.

Her back arches against my touch and I run my hand over her stomach, sliding two fingers over her wet clit to push them inside her. She moans and lifts her ass up off the bed, but she doesn't let me off the hook.

"You have money," she points out. "Lots of it, I think."

I kiss the vein in her neck and she pulls my hair, tugging my head back until I'm forced to look at her. I can tell she wants to ask what my parents do for a living, but I don't feel like talking about that while I'm finger fucking her, which is why I decide to distract her with my tongue. I lick the valley between her breasts and she whimpers, automatically rolling her hips out to fuck my hand.

"Good girl," I whisper, stealing another kiss from her mouth before I move down to lie between her legs. "Get up on your elbows and watch me eat your pussy."

"Jesus, Xan," she hisses, her cheeks flushed, but I think she likes it when I talk like that.

I dip my head and slide my tongue over the inside of her thigh, smirking to myself when she glares and knocks my head with her knee to get my mouth where she wants it. I curl my fingers inside her and kiss the edge of her pussy, teasing her like that a minute, then I give her what she wants and lick her clit until she forgets how much she doesn't like me.

"Holy shit," she chokes out, quickly slapping a hand over her mouth to stop herself.

I laugh lightly and reach up to take that same hand, moving it down to my head so she can run her fingers through my hair. She scrapes her nails over my scalp and I run my piercing over the ball of her clit, enjoying the quiet noises leaving her throat while she pushes my face down to her pussy.

She's holding out on me and I know it, but I don't rush her or tell her to come.

I'd eat her out all night long if she'd let me.

I slide my free hand over her stomach and pinch her nipple, rolling it between my thumb and forefinger. Her moans get louder and she tilts her head back on her shoulders, tightening her grip on my hair while she locks her thighs around my head. My scalp stings and I groan, fucking loving the way she tastes while she comes all over my fingers. I lick the wetness from her pussy and she pushes my head away, falling down on her back with her hair spread out like a messy halo around her head.

Funny considering I'm about to fuck the angel right out of her.

She grins like she knows it and I grin back, squeezing her hip while I run my tongue over the curve of her waist. I plan on licking every inch of her body until she's begging me for my cock, but then she sucks her stomach in and I look up at her, not missing the way I can see her fucking ribs poking out beneath her flesh.

"Stop doing that."

"Doing what?" she asks, frowning when I move up to crowd her space.

"That." I flick her navel, brushing her hair behind her ear when I catch the sadness in her eyes. "Fuck, baby, don't you know how perfect your body is?"

She hesitates, then slowly shakes her head no. I grind my teeth together and snatch her jaw to stop her, gently moving my hand to the back of her neck to hold her forehead against mine.

"Breathe out."

She doesn't, and I swear to god I could kill Noah fucking Campbell.

"Please, Jordyn."

She swallows but eventually does as she's told, looking so unsure that my heart physically aches for her.

Right then, I decide I'm keeping her for myself, mostly because I want to but also because *fuck this*.

She doesn't need those nasty motherfuckers filling her head with this bullshit.

Not now she has me.

"Xan?"

"What, baby?"

"I hate it when you call me Jordyn."

I raise a brow at that, dipping my head to tease her mouth with mine. "Same way you hated it when I licked your pussy just now?"

She nods and I smirk, slowly running my fingers over her stomach to slide one inside her. Her hips buck and I pin them with mine, twisting the hand between her thighs to add a second one.

"I wanna put my dick in here, princess," I tell her, rubbing my jeans against her inner thigh to show her how hard she makes me. "You gonna let me?"

She nods again and I move to grab the single condom I keep in my wallet, looking up at her when she takes my hand to wrap her fist around the packet.

"What?"

"I.." she trails off, rolling over onto her side to grab something from the drawer of her nightstand.

I frown and lean over to watch what she's doing, smiling to myself when I spot the single key attached to the purple devil keyring I left on her car a few weeks ago. She pushes my head away when she catches me looking and shuts the drawer, lying down on her back to pass me a piece of paper.

"What is this?"

"I got tested after I found out Noah cheated on me," she explains, chewing her lip like it's something she needs to be embarrassed about. "I, uh.. I'm on the shot."

"Jordyn," I warn, damn near going off in my jeans at the thought of what she's offering me.

"Have you ever done it without a condom before?"

"No, but I haven't been tested in a few weeks."

She nods and sits up a bit, reaching down between her legs to push my jeans down over my cock. "It'll be fine."

"Are you s–"

"Fuck, please, Xan," she cuts in, dropping her eyes to run her thumb over the tip. "I wanna feel it."

God fucking damn her.

I toss the paper away without looking at it and push her down on her back, quickly shedding the rest of my clothes before I retake my spot between her legs. I lean up on one elbow beside her head and fist the base of my cock, rubbing it over her pussy a few times to get it wet. I purposely slide my piercing over her clit and she moans, eagerly lifting her ass off the bed in an attempt to get the tip in. I pull it back a bit to deny her and take her mouth with mine, enjoying the impatient little growl leaving her throat.

"Xan–"

I shove it inside her with one hard hit and she screams, roughly digging her nails into the back of my neck to attack my tongue with hers. I groan at the feel of her and slide my hand beneath her ass, squeezing the soft flesh there to fuck her a little deeper.

"Oh my god," she cries out. "Shit."

I nod my agreement and suck on her bottom lip, fucking loving the way her bare pussy feels wrapped around my cock. Her tight walls clench around me and I tighten my grip on her ass, squeezing my eyes shut when I realize she's about to come already.

"Fuck, Jordyn," I grit out, riding her through it the best I can without going off like a thirteen year old virgin.

She finally stops shaking and I crack my eyes open to look at her, laughing lightly when I catch the surprise on her face.

"How did you do that?"

"Baby, I didn't do it on purpose."

"Damn," she whispers, not even bothering to hide the big ass grin on her face. "I like your friend Justin."

I shake my head at her and she runs her hands over my chest, shoving me back a bit to get me to move. I take the hint and drop down on my back beside her, taking her waist with one hand to guide her on top of me. At first I think she wants to ride me, but then she shuffles down to kneel between my legs and wraps her tiny hand around the base of my cock.

"What are you doing?"

"I wanna suck your dick," she says simply, dipping her head to swirl her tongue around my piercing.

Jesus Christ.

I knock my head back against the headboard and she laughs at me, opening her mouth to take me in as far as she can without choking on it. I'm a fucking pussy for this girl and I'm about to come down her throat, which is why I gather her hair into a makeshift ponytail at the top of her head and pull, grabbing my cock with my free hand to tap her bottom lip with it.

"Stick your tongue out for me."

She does and I slide it over the top, choosing a spot in the middle about two centimetres from the end.

Right there.

That's where I'll put it.

"What are you thinking about?"

"Piercing your tongue," I admit, smirking when her brows jump in horror.

"Excuse me?"

"You heard me."

She scrunches her nose and I pull her into me, brushing my lips against hers while I lift her up to straddle my hips. I line my cock up with her pussy and she sinks down on it, leaning over me to wrap her hand around my necklace. She grinds on me and I fuck up into her, sliding my hands over her sides to squeeze her waist.

"What's the key for, princess?"

"None of your business," she teases, squealing when I flip her over to lie on her back. "*Xan!*"

I shove my dick back inside her and spit on my thumb, moving it down between us to rub her clit. That sets her off and she moans, damn near ripping my hair out while she pulls my face down to hers.

"Baby," I rasp. "Your pussy feels so fucking good."

She whimpers and I dip my head to kiss her, but it's not a sweet kiss. It's wild and crazed and needy as fuck, and it doesn't take long for her legs to start shaking again.

"Fuck," she curses, throwing her head back when I increase the pressure on her clit.

I fuck her harder and slide my tongue over the edge of her jaw, moving down to dig my teeth into her neck. I suck on the sensitive flesh there but stop myself before I mark her, knowing she'll go off on me if she wakes up with a hickey in the morning, but then she cries out and tightens her grip on my hair, holding me down on her like she's begging me not to stop. I groan against her and she comes again, clenching her thighs around me in a way that drives me crazy. Her pussy squeezes my cock and I couldn't hold out if I wanted to. I pin her hips with mine and come inside her, falling down on her with one elbow propped up beside her head. Our heavy breathing mixes together and she stares at me, gently running her nails over the back of my neck.

"Is this the part where you run out on me and never talk to me again?" she jokes, but I don't miss the vulnerability right there beneath the surface.

"Tell me you lost on purpose."

She frowns at that, pulling her head back to bounce her eyes between mine. "What?"

"The game, princess," I remind her, lifting my hand to run my thumb over the vein in her neck. "Tell me you wanted this. Tell me you wanted *me*."

She cocks her head and opens her mouth to say something, but then her phone goes off somewhere beside us and she looks that way, leaning over the edge of the bed to grab it off the floor. She taps the button to stop the timer and sets it down on her nightstand, hesitating a second before she turns to look at me.

"Sorry, new boy," she teases, pulling a pink throw blanket over her chest while she moves in to speak over my lips. "Looks like you're shit outta luck."

Little Devil

15

Jordyn

"JJ?"

I groan my annoyance and crack my eyes open, squinting into the soft light of my bedroom to check my surroundings. Memories of last night come rushing back to me and I lift my head from the solid chest I've been sleeping on, slapping a hand over my mouth when I realize what's happening. I'm naked, *he's* naked, our bodies tangled in the sheets with his arms wrapped around my waist and my thigh wedged between his.

"JJ!" my mother calls again, knocking louder this time. "I know you're in there. Why is your door locked?"

Oh, shit.

"Just a second, Mom," I call back, giving myself exactly three seconds to wake up and think of a plan.

I smack Xander's chest to get him to move and jump out of bed, quietly running to my bathroom to grab my silk robe from the hook on the back of the door. I throw it on over my shoulders and scramble to collect our discarded clothes from the floor, throwing them into my closet before shutting the door to hide them. I turn around to check the room and tie my robe around my waist, gritting my teeth at Xander when I catch him grinning at me with his arms folded beneath his head and his hard dick resting on his stomach.

Fuck me, he's.. dead.

So fucking dead if my mom catches him in here.

He opens his mouth to say something and I grab a fist full of his hair, pushing him off the bed to drop him down behind it. "Stay there."

"Fuck, ow, baby–"

I smack him again to shut him up and cover his body with the blanket, quickly tossing the unused condom from the mattress before I move to open the door.

She's *never* home on weekends, barely even here on weekdays, and yet the one time she decides to show up at my bedroom at nine am on a Sunday morning just so happens to be the one time I'm hiding a boy in here.

The same boy I let fuck me senseless last night after knowing him for exactly three weeks.

Fucking hell, this is mortifying.

"I've been calling you for ten minutes," my mother says, dressed in a knee length navy blue dress with her hands propped on her hips. "Why aren't you up yet?"

"Sorry," I say lamely, leaning my shoulder against the doorframe to block her view of my bed.

"What happened to your hair?"

"I, uh.. went to the beach last night," I admit, inwardly bracing myself for the fallout. "It got wet."

"In the *sea*?!" she screeches. "What on earth is wrong with you? Do you know how disgusting that is?"

"It's just salt water, Mom," I mutter, self consciously lifting my hand to finger the tangled ends. "It'll be fine as soon as I wash i–"

"Don't bother," she cuts in, pulling her phone out from her purse to tap away on it. "I'll call Gabriella and have her come by to give you a deep condition. She can color your roots for you while she's here. You should have had those done two weeks ago, at least."

My jaw ticks and I cross my arms over my chest, silently watching her while she makes her call.

I'm naturally blonde so you can barely see my roots unless you look *really* closely, but I don't bother defending myself against the never wrong Elizabeth James.

I already know how that game works, and I never win.

She hangs up on our stylist and I glance over my shoulder, discreetly checking Xander's still out of sight before turning back to her. "Are you here to stay?"

"No, I just wanted to talk to you about this Washington nonsense before I leave for New York this afternoon. Are you free for an early lunch at eleven thirty?"

I swallow and blink the stupid tears from my eyes, mindlessly nodding my agreement. "Sure."

"Don't look at me like that, JJ," she huffs, rolling her eyes in annoyance. "A career in phot–"

"*Mom*," I hiss, reluctantly telling her what she wants to hear to shut her up. "I'm working on my application essay to Princeton, okay? I'm doing everything you've asked of me. Can we please just talk about this later?"

"Why are you acting so strange?"

"I'm not," I lie, but my cheeks are on fire and I wouldn't be surprised if she could see my pulse hammering against the side of my neck.

"I talked to Noah last night," she informs me, scanning my face to check my reaction. "He told me there's a new boy at school who's been bothering you, *harassing* you, even. Is that true?"

Jesus Christ.

"No."

"Are you sure?" she asks, clearly not buying it. "Because we can always get a restraining order if it's an issu–"

"Mom, stop," I plead, wishing the ground would open up and swallow me whole. "There's no issue, I promise."

She stands up a little taller and runs her tongue over her perfectly straight veneers, slowly moving her eyes over my form to check for the lie. "Fine." She nods, thankfully letting it go. "Gabriella will be here in an hour. Let her curl your hair and do your make up for you, then meet me downstairs at eleven fifteen. I'll have a car waiting outside to take us to lunch."

"Okay," I say quietly, forcing a small smile to please her because that's what good daughters do.

She finally leaves and I release the breath I was holding, locking the door again just in case she decides to come back for something else. I tighten my robe around my waist and walk around to the other side of my bed, laughing lightly when I find Xander lying down on his back with his head propped up on my nightstand and his hand on his dick.

"Come sit on my lap, princess."

"Not a chance, new boy." I shake my head, grabbing the blanket off the floor to toss it down on my mattress. "You need to leave."

He feigns a pout and moves to stand right in front of me, so close his dick pokes my navel through the silk. "You okay?"

"Why wouldn't I be?"

He shrugs and lifts my chin up with his forefinger, clearly unsure what to say. "Your mom seems.."

"Nice?" I offer, making him laugh.

"Yeah, *that*."

"Xan?"

"What, baby?"

"Why are you still naked?"

"Because you tossed my clothes in your closet," he reminds me, staring at my lips while he swipes his finger over the bottom one.

"Oh. Right." I clear my throat, walking away to grab them for him.

He uses the bathroom quickly and then sits down on my bed to pull his jeans on, eyeing me from beneath his lashes when he catches me staring at him. "What?"

"You slept over."

"I know."

"You do that with all the girls you go home with?"

"No," he says simply, standing up to pull his shirt on over his head. "I mean, there was this one girl a few weeks ago but it was a complete accident. I asked her to leave as soon as I realized she was still there and she punched me in the mouth. Then her older brother punched me in the nose and gave me the black eye I came with when I moved here. Fuckin' asshole."

My brows jump and I scrub a hand over my mouth, attempting to hide my laugh but failing.

"You think that's funny?"

"No."

He raises a brow and steps closer to me, sliding his hands around my waist to pull me into him. "I wanted to take you for breakfast."

"Why?"

"I don't know." He frowns, seeming just as confused by the fact as I am. "Wanna bail on your *nice* mom and sneak out with me instead? I'll buy you pancakes."

I grin and shake my head at him, taking his hand in mine to lead him over to the door. I look both ways to check the coast is clear and then pull him out into the hall, secretly wishing I could make whatever this is between us last a little longer. I can't do that, though, and I'm not naïve enough to believe he won't move on to someone else now that I've given him what he wanted. My stupid heart aches a little bit at the thought but I shut that down just as quick as it came.

Xander Reid is a player.

A bad boy who's low key dangerous and *not for me*.

I have to remember that.

We get to my front door and he pulls me out with him, hiding me behind his body while he brushes the hair back from my collarbone. "Don't be mad," he says. "But there's a tiny little hickey on your neck right there."

"What?!" I whisper yell, lifting my hand to cover the spot. "Why the hell would you do that to me?"

"I tried to stop it," he chuckles, pulling my hand away to run his thumb over the mark. "You wouldn't let me, remember?"

My cheeks burn and I smack his chest, narrowing my eyes when he continues to laugh at me.

"I hate you so much."

"I don't believe you," he teases, leaning over me to crowd my space. "Can I have your number?"

"No."

"Can I have a kiss?"

"N–"

He grabs my waist and pulls my hips to his, slowly locking his arms around my back to hold me against him. "I dare you."

I roll my eyes and snatch his jaw, pulling his face down to mine to give him what he wants. I tell myself to kiss him once and walk away like I did in the school parking lot that first time, but my stupid body seems to be acting on her own. I open my mouth for him and he takes the mile, sliding his tongue over mine like he's trying to ruin me from the inside out. His piercing makes me moan and I wrap my hands around his neck, but then my mother's raised voice rings out from somewhere inside the house and I jump, pulling away from him to wipe my mouth with my hand. He winks at me and I shove his ass, turning around to walk back inside before he catches the grin on my face. I shut the door and fall back against it, tipping my head back on the wood to touch my lips with my fingertips.

Goddamn him.

Little Devil

16

Jordyn

"I want details," Kian says, dropping down beside me at our top table at the back of the huge cafeteria.

"No."

"But, babe," he whines the word, pouting dramatically in true Kian fashion. "I thought I was your best friend."

I raise a brow at that, taking the bottled water he passes me to twist the cap off. "Since when?"

"Since Penelope's a whore and I'm the next best thing," he jokes, stealing a baby tomato from my plate to toss it into his mouth.

"Don't call her a whore, Ki."

"Ugh, you're such a good person," he complains, scrunching his nose in mock disgust. "I would've bitch slapped her by now if I were you."

"If you found out she was fucking Trav, you mean?"

His jaw ticks and I smirk to myself, taking my fork from my plate to finish eating my salad.

That was a cheap shot on my part, I know, but at least it steals his attention away from me.

For all of thirty seconds.

"Are you really not gonna tell me what happened on your date with the hot bad boy?"

"I already told you nothing happened," I mutter, lying through my teeth because no one, and I mean *no one*, can ever find out about what we did on Saturday night.

"Oh, *really*?" he draws out, clearly not buying the shit I'm selling him. "Because–"

"Kian, beat it," a voice says from behind us, and Kian shuts his mouth, leaning back in his seat to look up at my ex-boyfriend over his shoulder.

"We're talking, Noah."

"No, *we're* talking, you're *leaving*," he says simply, tipping his chin to dismiss him. "Now."

Kian shakes his head at him and stands up to do as he's told, barely managing to hide the hurt on his face while he walks for the double doors on the other side of the room. I move to go after him but Noah snatches my wrist, hard enough to keep me here but not hard enough to hurt.

"Sit down."

"What the hell is wrong with you?" I hiss, pulling myself from his grip to glare at him. "You know how sensitive he is and you treat him like shi–"

"Shut up about fucking Kian, JJ," he grits out, swinging his leg over to straddle the bench seat beside me. "What's going on between you and Xander Reid?"

"Nothing," I answer, but I don't think he believes me.

"You need to stay away from him."

"And *you* need to stay away from *me*," I fire back, ignoring his comment completely. "Oh, and stop ratting me out to my mom while you're at it."

"I didn't *rat you out*," he argues. "She asked me how you were doing and I told her the truth."

In other words, she asked how the whole *us getting back together* thing is working out for him and he told her it's not, same thing that happened between me and her at lunch yesterday. The whole thing went exactly as I expected – she all but begged me to forgive him and got all pissy when I told her no, then she lectured me about college and the importance of image and I listened with my mouth shut tight, mindlessly picking at my food while daydreaming about Xander and everything we'd done together the night before.

"I meant what I said about Reid, JJ," Noah says quietly, his warning clear. "I've seen the way he looks at you and I don't like it. He's a freak."

"He's not a freak," I mutter, dipping my head to play with the hem of my skirt. "He's just.. different."

"Why are you defending him?" He frowns, pulling his head back when I say nothing. "Do you *like* him?"

I roll my eyes and stand to leave, done with this conversation because I don't like the answers to his questions. He lets me go without a fight and I walk out to the hall to find Kian, smiling at him when I catch him talking with Travis by his locker. Kian smiles back and Travis follows his line of sight, glaring at something over my shoulder with his jaw locked. He moves like he's about to do something but Kian stops him, blocking his path with a single hand on his abs. I leave them to it and make my way to my own locker, purposely avoiding any and all eye contact while I collect my books for my next class.

I feel like everyone's staring at me.

Like I'm walking around with a big ass sign on my back that reads *I fucked Xander Reid and I liked it.*

I know I'm probably being paranoid, but it doesn't help that the bastard himself keeps staring at me every time we cross paths, smirking at me with a look that says *I know what your pussy tastes like.*

It's distracting.

And hot.

And I'm pretty sure I never got my mind back after he stole it from me the other night because *shit.*

What is happening to me?

Just as I think it, the sound of his laughter rings out from somewhere beside me and I look that way, immediately wishing I hadn't when I spot him talking to Amy Brennan at the end of the hallway. My brows crash in the center and I blink, struggling to ignore the hollow pit forming in my stomach at the sight of them together. She's standing with her back to me and he's leaning back against the wall in front of her, looking down at her with his head cocked in amusement while she props a hand on her hip and flips her light blonde hair over her shoulder. She's Noah's younger cousin, the sheriff's daughter and our student body president, the perfect *good girl* for him to corrupt with his stupid tongue bar and his dirty mouth. He moves his eyes over her form and I let out a scoff, shaking my head at myself while I abandon my locker to go to the bathroom.

Of course I was nothing more than a body for him to fuck, a game for him to win before moving on to the next one.

I *knew* that and he never told me different, so I don't know why I'm so pissed about it.

I wash my hands at the bathroom counter and glare at my own reflection, angry with myself for allowing him to get to me like this. I'm fully on board with pretending he doesn't exist when I walk back out there because *fuck him*, but then someone slips in through the door and I force my features even, jumping out of my skin when two big hands grab my waist from behind.

"*Xan*!" I squeal, widening my eyes when he hurries me along to the biggest stall at the end. "Oh my god, you can't be in here!"

He ignores me and locks the door behind us, backing me up against the left wall to pin my body with his. My heart picks up and I stare at him, stupidly liking the way he looks with his black tie wrapped loosely around his neck and his white shirt hanging out of his pants.

"Hey," he says, gently tipping my chin up with his forefinger. "Why are you upset?"

"I'm not upset," I lie, crossing my arms over my chest to feign indifference. "And even if I was, it's none of your business. *I'm* none of your business."

"Is that right?" he teases. "You don't like me anymore?"

"I never liked you anyway."

He makes a humming sound and moves closer, slowly moving my hair from my neck to inspect the makeup covering the hickey he gave me. My cheeks burn with his eyes on it and I have to force myself to keep breathing, wishing he didn't affect me this way but loving it all the same.

He makes me feel alive and I crave it like a drug.

"I think you're a liar," he muses, and I almost agree with

him, but then I remember what he was doing five minutes ago and snap myself out of it.

"What happened to Amy?"

"Who's Amy?"

My brows dip and I look up at him, searching his face for the joke or the taunt, but there isn't one.

He really doesn't know who I'm talking about.

"She's the blonde girl you were talking to just now," I mutter, immediately regretting it when I catch the stupid grin on his face.

"Are you jealous?"

"Are you gonna fuck her?"

His grin widens and he rests his forearm on the wall above my head, crowding my space with his height and his body and those magnetic hazel eyes that make me want to melt for him.

Stop it, JJ.

"She saw me smoking in the parking lot after last period and threatened to tell my aunt," he explains, looking me dead in the eye while he traces a finger over my bottom lip. "I don't want her, baby. She's got nothing on the way I feel about you."

"How do you feel about me?"

"Like I wanna kiss you until you can't breathe."

My mouth parts but I snap it shut again, confused and a little turned on by his unfiltered honesty.

I, however, have none of that.

"I don't want you to kiss me."

"You sure?"

I nod once, but he doesn't push me like I expected him to. Instead he cocks his head and backs away from me, reaching back to unlock the door behind him. I raise a brow and watch him open it, running my tongue over the spot he was just touching while I prepare myself for him to walk away.

A part of me knows he's bluffing, testing me to see what I'll do about it, but the other part is terrified he's actually done with me, and I don't like that part.

Without thinking too much into it, I snatch his crooked tie and yank him into me, quickly wrapping the fabric around my fist to speak over his lips. "If you tell anyone about this, I'll ruin your life."

He smirks at that, holding my eyes while he drags my thigh up to his waist. "Maybe I'll ruin yours."

And fuck me, maybe he will.

I pull his mouth down to mine and he groans, sliding his hand up beneath my skirt to squeeze my ass. My hips buck and I arch my back out for him, eagerly raking my hands through his hair while he rubs his body against mine. He makes good on his word and kisses me until I run out of air, then he moves his mouth to my jaw and down to the crook of my neck.

"Do you know how many times I've thought about fucking you in this uniform?" he asks, hooking his finger beneath my thong to pull it to the side.

"You're not fucking me right here."

"Later, then," he rasps, almost pleading. "Leave it on and meet me after school so I can get my dick back inside you."

I moan and open my mouth to tell him I'll do whatever

he wants, but then two familiar voices fill the space on the other side of the door and I freeze, pulling back an inch to look at Xander. They probably don't realize anyone's in here because the lock is disengaged, but all it would take is for one of them to lean over and spot two sets of feet beneath the door.

"How long do think it'll be before he gives up on her?" Penelope asks, making Sienna laugh.

"Why, because you want him all for yourself?"

"You know I do."

"Yeah, well, maybe she'll move on with someone else and he'll finally leave her alone."

"Move on with who?"

"I don't know," Sienna mutters. "I know the new boy likes her, though. Maybe she'll give in and date him."

Penelope snorts at that, loudly. "Don't be an idiot, Si. JJ wouldn't touch that freak with a ten foot pole. She's too far up her own ass to mess around with a guy like that."

Xander smirks at me and I smirk back, taking the hand between my legs to move it down to my pussy. He slides two fingers inside me and I tighten my grip on his hair, pulling him in to encourage him to kiss me again.

"You love this, don't you?" he whispers, so quiet I can barely hear him. "Me getting you off when you know we could get caught any second now. It makes you wild."

I nod and he drags my bottom lip out between his teeth, simultaneously rubbing my clit with his palm to set me off. The girls continue to talk shit about us but I don't care, I'm too focused on him and the way he plays my body like a song. He squeezes my outer thigh with his free hand and quickens his pace, shoving his tongue into my mouth while he pushes me over the edge. My orgasm hits me hard and I dig my nails into the back of his neck, shamelessly riding his hand to get it to last as long as possible.

"..and– wait, what was that?"

Sienna's question startles me and I cling to Xander with my heart in my throat, careful not to make a sound while my pussy throbs with the aftershocks.

"Bitch, you're hearing things," Penelope decides, followed by the sound of their heels tapping along the floor with their exit.

I let out a long breath of relief and lean back against the wall, reaching down to run my hand over his cock through his pants. It jerks beneath my touch and I pull his zipper down, crouching down in front of him to rest my ass on my thousand dollar stilettos. He curses and I take his dick out of his boxers, swallowing him down in one quick move to get it wet with my saliva. His forehead hits the wall above me and I open my mouth, working the base in my hand while I slide my tongue over the tip. He looks down at me and I lick the underside, proud of myself when a strangled out groan escapes his throat.

"God fucking damn, baby," he whispers, wrapping my hair around his fist to pull my head back a little further. "I can't fucking stand the way you look right now."

I grin and his cock pulses in my hand, his hot release shooting out across my tongue and down to the back of my throat. I swallow it all and suck him dry, laughing lightly when he jerks and pulls away from me. He helps me up to my feet and kisses the shit out of me, seemingly unbothered by the taste of his own cum.

"Give me your number," he pleads, breathing hard against my lips. "Don't say no."

Little Devil

I nod and he takes his phone out to pass it to me, kissing my collarbone while I hold it behind his head to do as I'm told. "Why didn't you just get it from Travis?"

"Because that's cheating," he teases, licking his way up to my earlobe to bite it.

I moan and wrap my hands around his neck to enjoy the attention, but then the first bell rings and I jump, pulling away from him to lift my hand up to my throat.

"I didn't give you a hickey," he assures me, somehow reading my mind without having to ask.

"Thank you."

He hides a grin and I roll my eyes, passing his phone back while I move around him to unlock the door. I walk out of the stall and check myself in the mirror above the counter, thankful my hair and make up still looks half decent despite what just happened. I quickly fix my lip gloss and throw my things back into my purse, side eyeing his reflection while he leans back against the doorframe behind me with his hands shoved into his pockets.

How he can act so calm when I'm damn near shaking right now is beyond me, but I don't call him out on it.

"Wait thirty seconds and then follow me."

"Whatever you say, princess."

I resist flipping him off and walk out into the hall, rushing back to my locker to grab the books I need. I get to my next class with less than a minute to spare and take my designated seat, more self conscious than ever over that imaginary sign on my back. Kian raises a brow at me but I pretend not to notice, determined to act casual while I flip to a clean page in my notebook to write the date at the top.

"Where have you been?"

"I had to run out to my car."

He makes a noise that suggests he doesn't believe me and I tighten my grip on my pen, looking up from beneath my lashes when I spot Xander walking through the door. He winks at me and drops down at his desk beside Travis, lazily leaning back in his seat with his long legs spread out wide. I shake my head at him and face forward again, cringing to myself when I hear my phone buzzing in my purse. I don't think the teacher heard it, though, so I lean over to grab it and hide it beneath the table to check the message on the screen.

Unknown: I want you bent over the hood of my car with your skirt flipped up over your ass.

My mouth parts and I dip my head, unable to stop the stupid smile spreading across my face. A minute passes and I consider ignoring him, but then I find myself saving his number and texting him back.

Jordyn: When?

Xander: I'll pick you up at four.

Xander: Ditch the thong, too.

I look up at that, chewing my lip when I catch him staring at me from the other side of the room. I shake my head no and he smirks to himself, discreetly looking between me and his phone while he types away on it.

Xander: I dare you.

Of course he does.

… Devil

17

Xander

"Where are you taking me?" she asks, still clinging to the door handle like her life depends on it, but at least she doesn't look as pissed at me this time.

"I don't know yet."

Her brows dip but she keeps her mouth shut, using her free hand to sip the iced coffee I gave her when I picked her up just now. At first I thought she'd tell me she doesn't drink that shit, but she took it with a smile and downed more than half of it before I hit the highway.

"You like that?"

She nods and sucks the life out of it until there's nothing left but ice, making me laugh. I keep driving without a destination in mind and she sits in comfortable silence for a while, leaning her head back on the seat to watch the scenery pass us by. After another twenty minutes, I choose a random exit and get off, smirking to myself when I spot the dead end sign up ahead. I make the turn and slow to a stop at the end of the road, dipping my head to get a look at the highway bridge above the small lake in front of us.

"Where are we?"

"Does it matter?" I tease, leaning over the inner console to run my finger over her bare thigh.

"It's pretty."

"*You're* pretty," I tell her, grinning when she turns her head to look at me.

She's still wearing her uniform, her buttons done up all the way to the top with her hair falling over her shoulders in perfect waves. I slide my hand up a little higher and she shivers, snatching my wrist to stop me while she looks around to check no one can see.

"It's just us, princess," I say quietly, taking her hand in mine to link our fingers together.

I kiss each of her knuckles and she chews her bottom lip, reaching down between us to unclip her seatbelt. She leans over to tease my mouth with hers and I move my hand down to her ass, groaning quietly when I realize she's taken her thong off like I told her to.

"So fucking bad for me," I whisper, gently dragging my short nails over her soft flesh.

A sexy little whimper escapes her throat and she pushes my chest, climbing over to straddle my thighs on the drivers seat. I squeeze her tiny waist and she runs her fingers through my hair, pulling my head back to take my mouth with a desperate kiss that drives me crazy. I bite her lips and she grinds on my lap, jumping when she accidentally hits the horn with her ass. I chuckle and wrap one arm around her back, blindly reaching for the door handle to carry her out. I walk around to the front of the car and lie her down on the hood, leaning over her to loosen the knot in her tie. I pull it off and pop the buttons on her shirt, kissing her throat while I push it down over her shoulders. She wiggles her way out of it and tosses it to the side, wrapping her legs around my waist to pull my body down to hers. Her mouth attacks mine and I let her own me for a while, fucking loving the way she drops her little *good girl* act for me and *only* me, but then she rubs her pussy against my zipper and I run out of patience. I pull back and flip her over to push her down on her stomach, pulling her waist down a little bit until her heels touch the gravel beneath us.

"Jesus, you were serious?"

"I'm not a liar, princess," I inform her, running both hands over the backs of her thighs to push her skirt up over her ass. "Spread your legs out for me."

She does and I slide my finger over her clit, damn near losing my mind when I realize how wet she is already. I take my dick out and move my eyes over her body, pulling the folded piece of paper from my pocket to give it to her.

"What's this?"

"Read it."

She frowns but does as she's told, leaning up on her elbows to get a look at the test results I got back from the doctor yesterday afternoon. Her frown deepens and she turns her head to look at me over her shoulder, clearly unsure what to make of me.

"Did you do this for me?"

I nod, fisting the base of my cock to tease her entrance with the tip. "You gonna let me in bare again?"

"What if I say no?"

"You won't say no."

She smirks and I smirk back, slowly pushing it inside until my hips bump her ass. She winces at the stretch and fists her hands on the hood of my car, dipping her head to hide her face from me.

"Feel good?"

"Yeah," she rasps, but she's lying and I know it.

I laugh lightly and lean over her to tangle my fingers in her hair, gently pulling her head back to speak in her ear. "How many times did you fake it for him?"

She tenses at that, awkwardly shifting her hips beneath mine. "What?"

"It's okay, baby, you can tell me," I whisper, moving my mouth down to her neck to kiss her there. "I won't tell anyone."

"I.." she trails off, hesitating a second before she speaks again. "Almost always."

"Yeah?"

"Yeah," she echoes, lifting her hand to run her nails over my scalp. "The only time he ever got me off was when he fingered me and ate me out at the same time."

I lock my jaw and grind my teeth together, not liking the thought of anyone but me eating her hot little pussy until she comes. I move my hand down beneath her and rub her clit, pulling out a little bit just to push back in. Her breathing picks up and I grin against her neck, grinding on her to give her the friction she needs.

"I'm gonna make this good for you," I assure her, slowly

dragging my teeth over the shell of her ear. "Hold on to me and tell me if it's too deep, okay?"

She nods and tightens her grip on my head, fisting my hair to pull my mouth back to her neck. I give her what she wants and fuck her a little harder, sliding my tongue over the pulsing vein beneath her flesh. Her pussy squeezes my cock and she moans, arching her back out to fuck me back hit for hit.

"Good girl," I praise, lifting her up a bit to increase the pressure on her clit.

"Fuck, Xan," she pleads, tipping her head back on my shoulder. "I need more."

"You sure?"

"Yes."

"Do you trust me?"

"*Yes*," she cries out, and I smile to myself because I'm pretty sure she means that.

I lift my free hand up to my mouth and spit on my thumb, watching her closely for her reaction while I move it down to slide it over her asshole. Her entire body locks up and I'm almost sure she's about to tell me to fuck right off, but then I realize it's because she's coming.

"Holy shit, Xan," she whimpers, quickly snatching my wrist to dig her nails into my forearm. "Why the fuck are you stopping?"

I blink and roll my hips out again, simultaneously getting her off with my fingers while I ride her through it. She comes loudly and I groan at the sight of her, rocking into her a few more times before my cock goes off inside her pussy.

"Jesus," she rasps, falling down on the hood with her arms folded beneath her head.

I laugh lightly and pull out, quickly shedding my shirt to clean us both up with it. She moans happily and I lie down on my back beside her, sliding my arm beneath her waist to pull her into me. She rests her head on my shoulder and her hand on my abs, mindlessly walking her fingers over my skin while we watch the sunset in the distance.

"I thought you smoked," she says after a while, making me frown.

"What?"

"I've seen you smoking a few times now and you said Amy caught you in the parking lot today," she explains, lifting her head to look at me. "How come you didn't have one the entire night you were with me?"

"I only smoke when I'm bored," I tell her, leaning up on one elbow to face her fully. "Or drunk. Or sad."

"You get sad?"

"Well, no," I admit. "But I'm sure I'd smoke if I did."

She shakes her head at me and I run my finger over the edge of her bra, then across to the valley between her breasts and down to her navel.

"You wanna do something bad?"

"I'm pretty sure everything I do with you is bad," she jokes, making me laugh.

"Maybe," I agree, slowly moving my finger down to the waistband of her skirt at her hip. "But being bad with me feels pretty damn good, right?"

She hides a grin and I kiss her lips, standing up to walk

around to the trunk. I open it up and move my gym bag to the side, leaning over to reach for the other duffel I keep in here. I pull it out and grab my jacket from the back seat, side eyeing Jordyn when she leans over to get a look inside the bag. Her mouth parts and she stands up with her hands propped on her hips, bouncing her eyes between me and the huge wall of graffiti beneath the bridge.

"What do you think you're doing?"

"What's it look like?" I tease, tilting my head for her to follow me. "Come on, princess."

"Are you insane?" she hisses, snatching her shirt from the ground to throw it on over her shoulders. "You can't just do whatever the hell you want, Xan."

"Says who?"

"Oh, I don't know," she deadpans. "The *law*? *Society*?"

"Fuck society."

She rolls her eyes but follows me anyway, leaving her buttons undone while she watches me with her arms folded over her chest. I choose a blank space in the middle of the wall and hold my jacket over my mouth, using my free hand to paint a badass blonde girl wearing a black hoodie and a black snap back. I don't have much time considering it's almost dark out, so I keep it simple and skip the detail, quickly using a mixture of blue and white to get her eyes the right color. Jordyn continues to watch me with her brows dipped and her mouth open, unable to hide the clear mixture of confusion and shock on her face.

"How are you doing that?" she asks, speaking for the first time in over thirty minutes. "Is that me?"

I laugh lightly and paint the words *little devil* on her

hoodie, stepping back once I'm done to get a better look. "You like it?"

"Yeah," she whispers, eyeing me over her shoulder while she moves closer to the wall. "Are you an artist or something?"

"Or something," I tell her, taking her hand to pull her back to my chest before she gets too close to the fumes. "I prefer skin over paper."

"You mean tattoos?"

I nod and wrap an arm around her waist from behind, leaning over her to kiss her neck. "Your turn."

She hesitates, just like I knew she would, but then she shocks the shit out of me and takes the jacket from my hand. "Got any purple?"

I raise a brow and pass her what she asked for, watching her in amusement while she covers her airways and gets to work. The way she looks right now makes my dick hard, eager to push her back against the wall and wrap her legs around my waist, but I soon forget that when I realize she's painting the purple devil emoji. As soon as she's finished, she grins like a kid in a candy shop and spins to face me, tossing my jacket at my head when she catches the look on my face.

"Don't look so smug, new boy," she mutters, scrunching her nose at the mess on her fingertips. "It was the only thing I could think of under pressure."

"You ever gonna tell me what that key in your nightstand is for?"

"Maybe," she teases, stepping closer to run her hands over my chest, but I don't miss the way her expression suddenly falls like she's disappointed about something.

"What's wrong?"

"Nothing," she lies, sighing when I lift her chin to pull her eyes back to mine.

"Baby, tell me."

"It's just.." she trails off, chewing her lip while she decides what to say to me. "Wait here."

I frown and she goes back to the car to grab something, looking much happier when she walks back over to me with her phone in her hand.

"What are you doing?"

"Come here," she orders, ignoring my question.

I do as I'm told and she pulls me into her, taking my hand to lift my arm over her neck, then she locks our fingers together and holds her phone out in front of us.

"Damn it, you're too tall for me," she complains, moving in front of me to place her hands on my shoulders. "Can you pick me up?"

"You take your selfies pretty seriously, huh?" I taunt, grabbing the backs of her thighs to wrap them around my waist.

She flicks my nose to shut me up and holds her phone out again, leaning her forehead against mine while she tilts the camera to get the wall in the background behind us. She takes the picture and drops her eyes to look at it, smiling to herself in a way that hurts my fucking heart. I don't know what's happening right now, but before I can think too much into it, a police siren rings out from somewhere and Jordyn slaps a hand over her mouth, quickly looking from me to the graffiti on the wall and then down to the bag at my feet.

"Oh, fuck." She panics, jumping down to kick her shoes off like she's about to make a run for it. "Should I call my lawyer? How much jail time are we gonna get for this? Oh my god, my mom's gonna lose her shi–"

"Jordyn?"

"What?"

"They're up there," I inform her, trying my hardest not to laugh while I point up to the highway bridge above us.

"Oh," she says, breathing long and deep with her hands fisted on her hips. "I knew that."

I laugh for real this time and she flips me off, folding her shirt over her chest to hide her body from me while she walks back to my car.

"Baby, don't be mad," I call, still chuckling to myself while I grab my shit and move to follow her.

"Don't call me baby."

"Why not?"

"Because I don't like it."

I smirk and catch up to her to snatch her waist, pulling her into me to back her up against the passenger side door. "You're hot when you lie to me."

She feigns a glare and shoves me back, climbing inside to pull her seatbelt on over her body. I jump in next to her and she hits me with the silent treatment, but I don't miss the way she turns her head to the side to hide the amusement there.

Fuck, I love that look on her face.

I'm pretty sure what I feel for her borders obsession, an unfamiliar *need* to be around her as much as I possibly can.

I don't know how she's managed to rein me in like this when she doesn't even like me half the time, but I don't hate it, so I don't fight it.

I just hope she doesn't rip my heart out and take it with her when she decides she's done with me.

Little Devil

18

Jordyn

Kian fluffs my hair out for me and taps my ass, slinging one arm over my neck while we walk through Sienna's front door. Loud music and drunken laughter fills my ears and I look around, resisting the urge to roll my eyes when I spot Penelope grinding on Sienna in the middle of the living room while Noah watches from his seat on the couch. I'm pretty sure she's trying to make him hot for her and it looks like it's working, but then he looks my way and glares, slowly leaning forward with his elbows on his knees and his eyes on my form. My hair is dead straight, my eye make up a little darker and riskier than usual, and I'm wearing a short red dress with a low back line and two criss cross straps over my shoulders. Honestly, I picked it out at the mall today because I knew Xander would like it on me, but it seems my ex-boyfriend's not a fan.

"Remind me why I'm here again."

"Because you promised you'd learn to socialise more and play nice with your friends," Kian tells me, leading me through the house to take me to the makeshift bar set up in the kitchen.

"Right," I mutter, leaning back against the island to watch while he pours us a vodka soda each.

My phone buzzes in my purse and I pull it out to check it, playfully shoving Kian's head away when he cranes his neck to snoop over my shoulder.

Xander: Baby.

Xander: Fuck.

Xander: You look so hot it hurts.

My heart skips a beat and I look around, raising a brow when I find him standing on the other side of Sienna's kitchen with his phone in his hand and his eyes on me.

Jordyn: What hurts?

He smirks at that, looking me dead in the eye while he reaches down to adjust his dick in his jeans. My cheeks burn without permission and I fight a smile – I *really* fight it – but it seems I'm not as sly as I think I am.

"Did you fuck him?"

I instinctively straighten my spine at the sound of his voice, discreetly hiding my phone behind my back when I find Noah standing in Kian's space beside me.

"Because if you did," he goes on, leaning over me to get in my face. "If you gave him what belongs to me when you promised our parents I'd be the only one you'd ever let inside you, I might not like that."

"Is that supposed to be a threat?"

"Yes," he says simply, reaching up to run his thumb over the lip gloss on my mouth. "You're mine and you always will be. Isn't that right, sweetheart?"

"No, it's not right," I bite out, gritting my teeth while I knock his hand from my face. "I'm not *your* anything and I'm sure as hell not your *sweetheart*, either."

He glares at me again and I move to leave, locking my jaw when he snatches my arm and yanks me into him. My skin itches with his hands on me, and it takes everything I have not to shove him back and smack the shit out of him. Xander steps forward in my peripheral like he's about to do it for me and I wince, silently hoping he's not stupid enough to do anything to Noah in front of a house full of his loyal followers. It's one thing to threaten him and shove his ass to the floor in front of me alone, but to do something like that in front of everyone here would be a helluva lot worse. Noah Campbell will be the mayor of this town in a few years, just like his father is now and his grandfather was before him, and I wouldn't put it past them to slap an assault charge on the new boy just because they can.

Travis appears out of nowhere to push his cousin back and I look at Noah, bravely wrapping my fingers around his wrist to pry his hand from my arm. I don't know where this new found courage has come from, but it's right there for the taking and I'm rolling with it.

"Does your daddy know you're still fucking Penelope?"

He falters for half a second and I smirk like a bad bitch, purposely clicking my tongue at him with a slow shake of my head. I wasn't entirely sure before, but the answer's written all over his face. He's still fucking her and he has no intention of stopping, and if his father knew he's risking his chance of getting back together with me for a piece of ass, as he'd call it, the disgusting bastard he is, heads would roll and Noah's would be the first to go, followed by Penelope's and then her parents'. William Campbell doesn't handle embarrassment well, and unfortunately for Noah, I'm not above using it against him.

"If you do anything to hurt the new boy," I say quietly, leaning up to speak in his ear. "I might not like that."

Anger radiates from him in waves but I ignore it, casually taking my drink from the island while I move around him to walk away. As soon as I step outside, my anxiety peaks and I run a hand over my throat, nervously pacing back and forth alongside the giant heated pool in the back yard.

I don't know what's gotten into me lately, but I do know it's got everything to do with Xander Reid and the way he makes me feel when I'm with him.

I've never felt more trapped in this bullshit life since discovering what a little freedom tastes like.

I want more.

I want Washington.

I want *him*.

The thought hits me like a slap to the face and I stop walking, looking down when my phone buzzes in my hand with another text from him.

Xander: You okay, princess?

I chew my lip and look over my shoulder, smiling a little bit when I see him leaning back against the wall next to the back door. I want to go to him and tell him *no, I'm not okay, I'm a spoiled little rich girl who doesn't want the life she's been handed on a silver platter,* but we're not the only ones out here, so I decide to keep my distance and text him back instead.

Jordyn: I'm bored.

Kind of a half truth, but luckily for me, he doesn't feel

like calling me out on it.

Xander: Bored, huh?

Xander: Wanna smoke?

A rare laugh bubbles out of me and I glance up at him, completely unprepared for the stupid ass look on his face. He's staring at me like my goofy laugh is the best thing he's ever seen, and I won't deny it feels pretty damn good to be looked at like that.

He tilts his head and takes a slow step back, side eyeing me while he walks back inside and makes his way through the house. The thought of *not* going with him doesn't even occur to me, so I move my feet and follow him to the front door, quickly checking to make sure no one's looking before I slip outside. As soon as my heels hit the porch, he locks an arm around my waist from behind and I squeal, giggling like a dumbass while he carries me down to his car parked on the driveway. He hides us behind it and sets me down on my feet, turning me around to back me up against the passenger side.

"Hey."

"Hey," he says back, dipping his head to take my mouth with a kiss that steals my soul.

"I thought you wanted to smoke," I manage to say, but I still find myself wrapping my arms around his neck to pull him in closer.

"I changed my mind," he tells me, sliding his hands over my sides and down to my ass, curling his fingers beneath the hem of my dress. "Is this for me?"

"Maybe," I tease, grinning over his lips when I feel his hard cock poking me in my stomach. "Is *that* for *me*?"

"All for you, baby," he rasps. "Come with me."

"Where are you going?"

"Home."

"What? Why?"

"Because if I stay here, your future mayor's gonna lose a tooth and I'll be spending the night in a jail cell."

"Oh."

"Oh," he mocks my tone, stepping back to open the passenger side door for me. "Are you coming?"

"I.." I hesitate, my brows dipping while I look from him to the seat and back again. "I should go back inside."

He laughs lightly at that, casually resting his forearms on the top of the doorframe. "Get in the car, Jordyn."

I take a breath and look at the party over my shoulder, then I do exactly what he knew I'd do.

I get in the car.

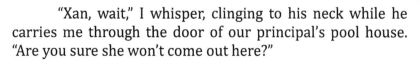

"Xan, wait," I whisper, clinging to his neck while he carries me through the door of our principal's pool house. "Are you sure she won't come out here?"

He nods and trips over something on his way to the couch, cursing the *pointless fucking step* while he sets me down on my back. He lies down between my legs and runs his hands over my breasts, groaning over my mouth when he realizes I'm not wearing a bra.

"Bad girl," he rasps, pulling my dress down to tease my nipple between his thumb and forefinger.

I arch my back out for him and he gives me what I want, slowly kissing his way from my mouth to my neck and then down to my chest. He licks me all over and I whimper, enjoying the way his piercing feels against my overheated skin. I run my fingers through his hair and he sucks on my nipple, watching me for my reaction while he slides his hand over my inner thigh.

"You want me to lick it?" he asks, pulling my thong to the side to touch my pussy with his knuckle.

I nod and he pushes my dress up over my ass, kissing every inch of bare skin he can find on his way down to the spot between my thighs. He *finally* gets there and I tighten my grip on his hair, moaning when his tongue bar slides over my clit in a way that drives me wild. I lift my ass up and he squeezes my hips, pushing me down to keep me pinned to the couch.

"You don't even need my fingers, do you, baby?" he asks, somehow knowing I'm on the edge without me having to tell him. "You gonna come on my tongue?"

I nod again and he quickens his pace, sucking on my clit every few seconds before he goes right back to licking me. My legs shake and I tip my head back on my shoulders, shamelessly holding his face down on my pussy while I fall apart for him. I trap his head between my legs and he eases me through it, slowly licking his way down to my inner thighs to kiss me there.

"So fucking hot," he praises, pushing my dress up a little further to expose my ribs.

My limbs feel like jello but I manage to pull it off over my head, lying back to enjoy the way he worships my body like it was made for him. He takes his time and I begin to squirm beneath him, moaning loudly when he sucks on the sensitive flesh beneath my hip bone.

"Goddamnit. *Xan*," I plead, snatching his jaw to pull his mouth back up to mine.

"What is it, princess?" he asks, his tone laced with mock concern. "You need my cock already?"

"You're such an asshole," I inform him, reaching down between us to pop the button on his jeans.

He smirks and pulls his dick out, holding my eyes while he slides the tip over my clit. He lifts his hips up and pushes his way inside me, moaning when I purposely tighten my walls around him.

God, that sound.

I do it again and he growls like a madman, linking our fingers together to pin my hands to the couch above my head. He smashes his mouth on mine and I bite his lips, roughly digging my nails into his knuckles to set him off. It works and he fucks me hard and deep, his cock piercing rubbing me just where I need it on every grind of his hips. It feels fucking amazing, his hard body pressed right up against mine while he takes me like he owns me. He's still fully clothed and I'm wearing nothing but my thong, the rough material of his jeans rubbing against my ass turning me on more than I ever thought possible.

"Fuck, Xan, I'm gonna come," I rush out, wiggling my hands from his grip to wrap them around his neck.

He pulls my head back by my hair and sucks on my tongue, pushing my legs out even further to get the angle he wants. My eyes roll back in my head and I come hard, shaking like a leaf beneath him while he rolls his hips into me. He stills on one final hit and drops his face to the crook of my neck, breathing hard against my flesh while his cum spills out inside me. My legs fall apart either side of him and I run my nails over his scalp, staring at the ceiling above us while I wait for my heart to slow down.

And I *really* need it to slow the hell down.

I'm fully aware this is just sex – a way for him to blow off steam or whatever it is fuck boys do in their spare time – but I'm still struggling to ignore that little kick in my chest that tells me this could be something more.

There is no more, you stupid girl.

I sigh on the inside and he kisses my collarbone, pulling back a bit to pull his t-shirt over his head. He cleans the cum from between my legs and I lean over to grab my dress from the floor, frowning when he takes it from my hand and walks away with it.

"What are you doing?"

"Getting you a shirt to wear," he tells me, grabbing yet another black one from his closet to pass it to me.

I stare at him in confusion and he winks, casually moving for the kitchen to grab something from the cabinet next to the sink.

"You want some popcorn?" he calls, popping the button on the microwave to toss a brown paper bag inside.

"Popcorn."

"Popcorn," he repeats. "It's that white stuff they sell at the concession stand in movie thea–"

"Xan."

He smirks to himself and I shake my head at him, anxiously chewing my lip while I drop my eyes to the shirt in my hand. He's still got my dress and I.. have absolutely no clue what to do with myself. Not wanting to continue standing here like a naked dumbass, I pull his shirt on over my head and step around the couch to go to him, jumping a fucking mile when I find a giant *animal* sitting at his feet with its paw on Xan's thigh.

"Jesus, what is that?!" I screech, quickly hopping up onto the coffee table like that'll protect me from it.

"*That* is my dog," he says simply, tossing it a couple treats from the little glass jar on the counter.

He has a dog?

"That's not a dog," I inform him. "That's a bear."

"He's not a *bear*," he defends, grinning down at him while he scratches his forehead. "He's cute as fuck."

"If you say so," I mutter, although he *is* kind of cute if you can ignore the nasty looking teeth and the paws as big as my fists. "What's his name?"

"Bear."

I blink at that, scrunching my nose when I catch the amusement on his face. "You're not funny."

He laughs at me and I look at the dog, jumping again when he steps forward like he's about to come by me. I move away and he barks at me, the fucker, opening his big ass mouth with a whine that has me squealing.

"What the fuck is his problem?!"

"You're freaking him out."

"*I'm* freaking *him* out?"

"He can sense your fear and he doesn't like it," he explains, taking my hand to guide me off the coffee table. "Sit your ass down and relax. He's the laziest dog on the planet. He won't hurt you, I promise."

I huff out a breath and force myself to do as I'm told, narrowing my eyes at Bear when he sits down in front of the couch and cocks his head at me.

"Boy could swallow me whole and he knows it," I mutter.

Xan snorts and passes me the remote for the TV, going back to the kitchen to grab the popcorn while I lean back to choose something to watch.

"Are we really gonna sit here and watch a movie together?" I ask, crossing my legs to rest my forearms on my thighs. "With your dog?"

"You got something better in mind?"

"Well, no, but.. don't you want me to leav–"

He appears on my left and I look up at him, shutting my mouth when he holds out what looks like a mug of hot chocolate with a shit load of whipped cream and mini marshmallows on top. Suspicion makes me pause and I pull my brows in, looking from him to the pile of snacks on the coffee table and then back to him again.

"Are you trying to make me fat?"

He stares at me for a solid five seconds, and then the asshole bursts out laughing. "Baby, *no*," he stresses, setting the drinks down on the coffee table to level with me. "Why would you ask me that?"

"I.." I shrug halfheartedly, lowering my voice with a mixture of shame and embarrassment. "I can't eat that stuff, Xan."

"Cant or you're not allowed?"

"Does it matter?"

"It matters to me."

"Why?"

He sighs and sits down in the corner beside me, gently pulling my legs over his lap while he wraps his arm around my waist. "I won't force you to eat anything you don't want," he says quietly, dipping his head to speak in my ear. "And no, I don't want you to leave. I'd keep you here every night if you'd let me."

I pinch my lips together and take the remote from the couch beside me, busying myself searching Netflix to hide the stupid emotion creeping up to the surface. I choose *The Conjuring* and he raises a brow at me, tilting his head at Bear to motion for him to hop up onto the couch beside us. He rests his chin on Xan's thigh and I hold my breath, silently waiting for him to rip my leg off with his teeth, but he doesn't do that. Instead he yawns and falls asleep almost immediately, seemingly enjoying the way Xan thumbs the spot between his eyes.

"You like horror movies?" he asks, leaning over me to grab the bowl of popcorn from the table.

I nod, hesitating a second before I decide to tell him something I've never told anyone. "I like anything with blood or sex. Or both. Same goes for books."

"Books."

"Books," I repeat. "They're those chunky things you can get at libraries. Kinda like movies but on paper."

"Fuckin' smartass," he chuckles, lightly jabbing his finger into my ribs.

I snort and sip my hot chocolate, resisting the urge to moan because *damn, this tastes good.* The movie starts to play and I rest my head on his shoulder, making sure to keep my hands away from Bear just in case he changes his mind and decides to eat me. Xander tightens his arm around my waist and I tease his abs with my fingertips, enjoying the shudder running through his body. At first I think it's because of me, but then he mutters a curse and I look up at him, rolling my lips when I catch him hiding his eyes behind my head.

"Are you scared?"

"Nope."

I laugh at him and finish my drink, reaching up to run my nails through the hair at the back of his neck.

He's totally scared.

Little Devil

19

Jordyn

He slides his hand over my ribs and I shift on his bed, pushing my ass back into his lap to make myself comfortable. I'm still wearing his t-shirt and he's wearing nothing but his boxers, his hard cock pressed up against my pussy through the fabric of my thong.

"Are you awake yet?" he whispers, dipping his head to kiss the crook of my neck.

"No," I whisper back, making him laugh.

I crack my eyes open and he moves his mouth up to the shell of my ear, lightly dragging it out with his teeth. I moan happily and he moves his hand down to my inner thigh, slowly lifting it up over his lap. Just when I think he's about to get me off with his fingers, the dog barks from somewhere and Xan groans in my ear, reluctantly sliding out of bed to open the pool house door for him.

"Go on, you little cockblock."

Bear drags his feet while he goes outside and I

chuckle, stretching my arms up over my head to fold them behind the pillow. Xan leaves him to it and walks over to me, sleepily running a hand through his purple hair in a way that makes him look messy and bad and so fucking hot it hurts to look at him. He raises a cocky ass brow and I tense, inwardly preparing myself for him to ask me to leave, but he doesn't do that.

"Can I take you to breakfast after I walk Bear?" he asks, leaning over me to lie down between my legs.

"I.." I frown, quickly shaking my head to clear it. "I promised Kian I'd go out with him this morning considering I ditched him last night, remember?"

He pouts and kisses my lips, sliding off of me to walk over to the kitchen. "Coffee, then?"

I hesitate but nod, shamelessly watching his body while he grabs a couple mugs from the cupboard overhead. He leaves the coffee maker to do its thing and then heads to the bathroom, smirking to himself when he catches my eyes following his every move.

"You're hot, too, princess."

Goddamnit.

I bite my lip and sit up on his bed, sucking in a breath when Bear jumps up to sit next to me. He rests his chin on my lap the same way he did with Xan last night and I freeze, unsure what to do with my hands. I'm still terrified of him, but I don't miss the way he's barely moved in the twelve hours I've known him.

"You really are a lazy little shit, huh?" I mutter, slowly moving my hand up to touch his head with one finger.

He closes his eyes and I get a little braver, gently scratching the spot behind his ear. He falls asleep on me and I grin, leaning back against the headboard to take a look around. Xan keeps this place clean but a little messy, a few bits of clothing thrown here and there and his school books hanging around all over the place. I spot the picture on his nightstand and lean over to get a closer look, pulling my brows in when I realize he's got his arm wrapped around Niko Reid's neck. At first I think it's a little weird that he keeps a framed picture of him and a famous musician on his nightstand right next to his bed, but then I catch the resemblance between the two and my jaw hits the floor.

Is that his *brother*?

Alec Reid and Isla Montgomery's son?

That's.. not possible, surely, but Xan's last name is..

Just then, the bathroom door opens and he walks out, grinning like a kid in a candy shop when he finds me and his dog cuddled up in bed together. He goes back to the kitchen to finish the coffee and I stare at the side of his face, gently climbing out from beneath Bear to ensure I don't wake him.

"Hey, Xan?"

"Yeah, baby?"

"Did you ever watch that nineties movie with the priest and the call gir–"

He drops his spoon down on the island and I slap my hands over my mouth, desperately trying not to laugh when I catch the look on his face. He looks surprised and annoyed and amused all at once, his head cocked to the left while he leans back against the kitchen side.

"You think you're funny?"

"No," I lie, the words muffled by my hands.

He shakes his head at me and slides me my coffee,

eyeing me from beneath his lashes while he grabs his spoon to stir his own. "How did you find out?"

"Your brother was *Niko* freaking *Reid*," I inform him, pointing to the picture on his nightstand with a low key fangirl groan. "I love him so much, Xan."

"Awesome," he mutters, leaning his elbows on the island to level with me. "I'm the good looking brother, you know? He was the ugly one with all the talent."

"Of course he was, sweetie," I feign agreement, dropping down on the bar stool opposite him to sip my coffee. "Your parents are hot."

"Jordyn."

"Did you know there were rumours going around back then that their sex scenes were real? That he *actually* put it in her right there on se–"

He gags and I burst out laughing, taking my phone out from my purse with every intention of googling him. He swings around the counter and I squeal, quickly jumping up to run away from him. He catches me by the waist and bends me over the back of the couch, tickling my ribs until I'm screaming with laughter.

"Give it up, princess."

"Make me, rich boy."

He tickles me again and I thrash against him, freezing when my phone rings in my hand. I straighten my spine and tap the button to answer it, holding his face away with my free hand when he tries to kiss me.

"Kian, hey."

"Bitch, why didn't you text me back?"

"I, uh.. sorry, I haven't checked my messages yet."

"Okay, well, I'm leaving Travis' house now but I need to go home and grab my car real quick. Can I pick you up in a half hour?"

Shit.

"Um.." I hesitate, hiding behind Xan when I spot Kian walking up the driveway through the kitchen window. "I only just woke up. Can you make it an hour?"

"Okay, fine," he chuckles, lowering his voice before he speaks again. "Hey, JJ?"

"Yeah?" I ask, craning my neck to look at him.

"Tell your new boy I said sorry for stealing you away so soon," he teases, winking right at us before he slides into the passenger seat of Travis' car.

I drop my jaw and he hangs up on me, probably laughing to himself like the bratty little fucker he is while Travis drives him away. Xan snorts out a laugh and I smack his chest, narrowing my eyes when he wraps his arms around my waist to pull me into him.

"This isn't funny, Xan."

"I think it's funny."

"What if he tells someone?"

"Who cares if he does?"

"*I* care."

"He won't tell anyone."

"He'll tell Trav."

"Yeah, well, Trav won't tell anyone," he says simply, leaning over me to tease my lips with his. "You want me to give you a ride home?"

"No, it's okay, I'll text my driver to pick me up."

"Why?"

"Because you need to stay here and feed Bear," I remind him, tipping my chin at the bed where he's still fast asleep on his side. "And walk him."

He nods and presses his mouth to mine, sliding his hands over my back to squeeze my ass. "Promise you won't read any of those bullshit articles about me?"

"Nope."

He growls his frustration and I grin, backing away from him to grab my dress from the kitchen counter. I go to the bathroom to change and check my hair in the mirror above the sink, silently pleading with my stupid heart to stop *feeling* for the boy who's not mine.

Not mine, not mine, not mine.

But fuck, he feels like mine.

20

Xander

"Aren't you done yet?" I complain, folding my arms on the table opposite her to rest my chin on top. "I'm bored."

The bitchy librarian chick shushes me from her desk on my left and Jordyn fights a grin, sneaking a glance at me with a look that makes my dick hard. I've been sitting here for forty five minutes, watching her like a love sick moron while she writes whatever she's writing for this stupid Princeton essay she's working on. It was entertaining at first because she's so fucking pretty but now I'm getting agitated, not so patiently waiting for her to finish so I can lure her into a dark corner, pin her back against a bookshelf and drop to my knees for her.

I can't get enough of her and it's making me a little crazy, to say the least.

I've fucked a lot of girls since I lost my virginity to some faceless stranger the day of my brother's funeral, but none of them made me feel the way she does. I *liked* having her in my bed the other night, wearing my shirt, her hot body pressed right up against mine beneath the sheets.

I want more.

So much fucking more.

"Xan," she says quietly, not looking up from her laptop while she continues to tap away on it.

"Yeah, baby?"

"Why are you staring at me like that?"

"Because I'm obsessed with you," I say simply, enjoying the light laugh leaving her while she shakes her head like I'm joking.

"Are you trying to be cute?"

"Is it working?"

"Maybe a little bit," she admits, grabbing her pen to jot something down on a little yellow sticky note. "Just give me five more minutes and I'm yours, okay?"

I groan at the word *yours* and the librarian shushes me again, glaring daggers at me when I lift my hands up in mock surrender.

"Sorry," I call out, wincing when her glare deepens.

Oops.

Jordyn sighs and I shrug it off, reaching over to grab one of her black notebooks from the small stack beside her computer. I flip it open to a random page and she lifts her head, her blue eyes widening with something that looks an awful lot like panic.

"Xan, don't–"

But I'm already looking down.

"You take pictures."

"No."

"Yes."

"*No*," she repeats, snatching the book from me to shove it into her purse.

As soon as she's done grabbing her stuff, she makes a beeline for the door and I move to follow her, amused by her lame ass attempt to run away from me.

"Jordyn, wait–"

"Jesus, can you just stop?" she hisses, spinning around to face me fully.

"Stop what?"

"Whatever it is you're trying to do right now," she says through her teeth, blowing out an aggravated breath when she catches the confusion on my face. "You don't need to pretend to care about me and my life, Xan. I'm not your girlfriend."

"But I want you to be."

"I don't care what you want."

"What do *you* want?"

She blinks at that, frowning at me like I'm the only person who's ever bothered to ask her. "What?"

"You heard me," I tease, closing the small distance between us to crowd her space. "What do you want, Jordyn James?"

"I.." she trails off. "I don't.."

"Is it Washington?" I guess, somehow knowing she's not ready to say it herself. "You wanna go to Washington to study photography?"

She hesitates but nods once, chewing the inside of her

cheek like she's fighting tears.

"Baby, what's wrong?"

"I can't go, Xan," she whispers, and the sadness in her voice breaks my fucking heart in two. "My mom won't pay for Washington and they won't give me a student loan because she earns too much money. I can't get a bank loan because I don't have the credit or a full time job to pay it back. I'm going to Princeton."

The finality of her statement makes me feel sick and I take her face in my hands, gently swiping my thumb over her cheek to catch the single tear there.

"Xan.."

"Will you show me?" I ask softly, pulling her in to rest my forehead against hers. "Please?"

She stares at me and I'm almost sure she's about to tell me to fuck off, but then she steps back and tilts her head for me to follow her. I do and she looks around to make sure no one's watching us, discreetly heading for the back corner where it's less busy. As soon as we're out of sight, she takes my hand and leads me to the science fiction section, pulling me down to sit on the floor beside her. I lean back against the bookshelf behind us and she takes the notebook out of her bag, pointing a single finger at my face with a fake glare.

"If you laugh at me, I'll never fuck you again."

"I'm not gonna laugh at you," I assure her, wrapping my arm around her neck to kiss her temple. "Unless you suck *really* bad. Then I'll probably laugh at you."

She jabs her elbow into my ribs and I grin, taking the book she passes me to rest it on my lap. I flip it open and look at the first page, carefully running my finger over the picture of the stars in the night sky. The moon looks huge, almost like she zoomed on it as much as she possibly could, but somehow the picture still looks clear and bright and really fucking beautiful.

"How did you do that?"

"My camera was *really* expensive," she jokes, leaning into me to rest her head on my shoulder. "Keep going."

I do as I'm told and turn to the next one, finding page after page of cities and sunrises and *people* – several different people I've never seen before of all shapes and sizes, ages and races, most of them standing on the beach with the sun and sea behind them. I get to a page about a quarter of the way through and find two pictures side by side, one of a black woman posing in a dark green swimsuit with her hands on her wide hips and an awkward look on her face, then one of the same woman laughing her ass off with her head tipped back between her shoulders.

"What happened there?"

"I told her she's got a nice ass."

I laugh at that, rubbing my hand up and down over her arm while I turn to the next one. I don't know much about photography and editing and all that stuff, but I'm pretty sure these aren't photoshopped. She's *embraced* their imperfections, kept every curve and blemish and stretch mark and made these people look proud of themselves and the bodies they live in.

It's amazing.

She's amazing.

"Baby, these are incredible."

"Really?" she asks, sounding genuinely surprised by that.

"Yeah. *Really*," I stress, pointing to the one of the young couple rolling around on the sand together in their swimsuits. "What's their story?"

"I met the girl in Miami on spring break," she explains, grinning at the memory. "I was shooting her solo for a while and she kept looking at the guy behind me. I knew she thought he was cute so I called him over and told her to wrap his arms around her from behind. He did it and she looked like she wanted to die, but I kept going and they got really into it. It was awesome."

"They're *strangers*?" I ask, pulling my brows in while I look through their series of pictures. "They look like they're in love."

"Yeah, well, I don't know about love, but I'm pretty sure he took her back to his hotel room when I got done with them."

"Was he hard?"

"*So* hard," she laughs, making me laugh.

She relaxes against me and I take my time flicking through the rest, drinking up every ounce of information she offers me regarding the people she's met over the years.

"Do you give them the pictures?"

"Yeah," she answers, handing me another photo book to go through. "I take their contact information before they leave and get their permission to share them on social media, then I go home and send the pictures over from my computer, choose my favorites and post them to a separate Instagram account I made."

"Can I see?"

She chuckles at the eagerness in my tone and passes me her phone, resting her head on my shoulder while I scroll down through the account. She's using a fake name and a generic profile picture, but she's still got just over seven thousand followers and hundreds of comments on each post, some even asking how they can book a shoot with her. I don't know how much time I spend examining each photo she's taken but I can't seem to stop. Every little thing I learn about her makes me want her even more. Every thought she has, every memory, every secret.. I crave them like a drug. I want her to give me every last one of them so I can lock them up with my own and keep them safe for her.

"Did you apply yet?" I ask, looking over at her when she doesn't answer right away.

She shakes her head and fiddles with the hem of her pleated skirt – something I know she does as an excuse to look down when she's feeling nervous or embarrassed about something. "I'm not applying."

"What?"

"I'm not applying," she repeats, leaning forward to pack her books away.

"Why the fuck not?"

"Because," she sighs, doing everything she can to avoid my eyes. "If I don't get in, it'll break my heart to know I'm not good enough, and if I do get in, I won't be able to go. It's a lose-lose for me, Xan, and there's no point hurting myself over something I can't have."

"Baby."

"Xan."

"You're applying to that school."

"Oh, really?" she asks, finally lifting her head to raise that bratty little eyebrow. "You gonna make me?"

"Maybe," I tease, pulling her into me until she's straddling my thighs. "Maybe I'll pin you down and tease your needy little clit with my cock, deny you and make you beg me to put it inside you, then I'll smack your pussy and start all over again until you learn to listen to me and do as you're told."

"That sounds awful," she rasps, digging her freshly manicured nails into my neck to grind on me.

My cock thickens between us and I groan, squeezing her ass to encourage her to keep riding it. "When's the application deadline?"

"January fifteenth," she answers, dipping her head to tease my mouth with hers.

I kiss her and slide my hands up over her thighs beneath her skirt, smirking when she moans and shoves her tongue into my mouth to get to my piercing.

Five weeks.

Five weeks to convince my girl that it's okay to say *fuck it* and take what she wants for a change, to do what she loves instead of breaking her own back every damn day to give every other fucker what *they* want.

Judging by the way she's taking *me* right here in the corner of the school library in the middle of the day, though, I'd say I'm already half way there.

21

Jordyn

"Did you get it?" he asks, leaning over the inner console to push the passenger side door open for me.

I nod and jump inside, grinning at Bear over my shoulder while I pull my seatbelt on over my chest. He's sitting down on the back seat with his big ass tongue hanging out of his mouth and his eyes on me, seemingly excited to have me tag along for his weekly trip to the dog beach. He moves forward like he's about to lick my face and I scrunch my nose, leaning away from him as far as I can to ensure he doesn't touch me with it. Xan laughs at me and I flip him off, squealing when he hits the gas and speeds off through the open gate at the end of my driveway.

"Xan!" I screech, squeezing my eyes shut when he almost clips the side of a Bentley, but he just laughs some more and keeps going.

He drives like he's late for a dentist appointment, reckless and fast and fucking stupid, and even though I've gotten through several rides in the car with him without dying, I still fear for my life every single time.

"Why can't you just drive in a straight line and wait your turn like a normal person?"

"Where's the fun in that?" he jokes, reaching into the cup holder to pass me an iced coffee with a purple straw.

"Did you ask for extra syrup?"

"And crushed ice instead of cubed," he adds, smiling to himself when he catches me slurping it up like a coke fiend.

He likes buying me treats I can't have and I like having them, mostly because they taste good but also because *fuck it*, what my mother doesn't know won't hurt her.

"I bet if you sucked my dick like that I could come before we get there."

I choke on my drink and cut my eyes to his, quickly grabbing a napkin to wipe the spit from my chin. "That's not a dare, right?"

He snorts and shakes his head at me, casually resting his hand on my lap to run his thumb over my thigh. I'm wearing a tight pair of skinny jeans and the faded black hoodie I stole from him the other day, my hair tied up in a thirty second bun and my face free of makeup. I wouldn't usually look like this outside of the privacy of my own bedroom, but Xan has this weird ability of making me feel beautiful no matter what I wear. I'm pretty sure I could walk around with a brown paper bag shoved over my head and he'd still tell me how bad he wants to hold me down and fuck me stupid.

We get to the beach and he chooses a spot in the almost empty parking lot, then he climbs out to open the back door for Bear. He smiles at me while he grabs what he needs and I chew my lip, nervously running my finger over the strap on my camera. He told me to bring it and I told him I would, but now I'm feeling a little unsure.

No one's ever taken an interest in me the way he does and I don't know whether to love it or hate it.

The passenger side door suddenly opens and I look up, finding Xan standing over me with his arm resting on top of the door frame. He eyes me and I clear my throat, climbing out to hold my hand out to him.

"Can I walk him?"

He hides a grin at my obvious distraction tactic and hands me the leash, falling in line beside me while we walk down to the beach. "How fast can you run?"

"What?"

He takes my camera and opens his mouth to explain, but then Bear yanks me forward and makes a beeline for the ocean like a bat out of hell. I scream and stumble to keep up with him, tightening my grip on the leash to ensure I don't lose this fucking dog. He pulls me along to the edge of the water and I'm officially panicking, attempting to dig my heels into the sand to get him to slow down, but it doesn't work. He's too damn strong and my stupid legs won't move fast enough.

"Oh, shit!"

"Baby, just let him go," Xan calls from behind me, and I drop the leash to the ground, leaning over with my hands on my knees to catch my breath.

He appears at my side and I feign a glare, smacking his abs when I catch him laughing his ass off.

"You're not fucking funny," I bite out, straightening up to snatch my camera from his hand.

"I tried to warn you," he chuckles, heading over to Bear

to unclip the tangled leash from his collar.

As soon as it's off, he sprints along the shoreline to get his paws wet and then ventures in a little deeper, swimming right into the ocean until the water reaches his neck. We walk along the beach to keep an eye on him and I lift my camera to take his picture, grinning when I realize how good he looks with the sun setting on the horizon behind him. I feel Xan watching me the entire time but do my best to pretend he's not there, taking about a hundred pictures from every angle I can manage. We let him do his thing for a while and then Xan whistles to call him back, sighing when he runs out of the water and soaks us both with a full body shake.

"Thanks, man," he mutters, crouching down beside him to clip the leash back on.

I laugh quietly and take a picture of his back, biting my lip to hide my enjoyment while I snap a few of the two of them together. He stands up to his full height and I back away from them, secretly loving the way he walks towards me with his purple hair falling over his forehead and the chain wrapped around his hand. My camera likes him almost as much as I do, and I already know my followers are gonna lose their shit when I post these on my account later. He keeps moving towards me and I keep moving back, but then he steals the camera from my face and holds it out to the side.

"Hey."

"Kiss me and you can have it back," he teases, leaning over me to brush his nose against mine.

I shake my head at him and press my lips to his, blinking when I hear the click of my camera on my left.

"What do you think you're doing?"

"Showing you how happy you look right now," he says simply, turning the camera around to show me the picture he just took of us together.

I touch my lips to hide the smile on my face and he runs his hands over my sides, pulling me into him until my chest bumps his. I look up at him and he kisses me again, sliding his arms around my waist with something that feels an awful lot like possession.

He's kissing me like he wants to keep me.

And goddamn him, I think I want that, too.

Little Devil

22

Xander

I lean back against the door frame and chew my gum, shamelessly watching her move while she leans over my bathroom counter to put her lip gloss on. She wanted to take a shower when we got back from the beach just now and I needed to clean my messy bastard of a dog, but now I'm pissed at myself for missing the opportunity to fuck her in there. She looks equal parts angel and devil wearing a white lacy thong and a matching bra, her towel dried hair falling over her back in subtle curls that reach the curve of her spine. *Slow Down* by Chase Atlantic plays through the speaker on the counter and she turns it up a little bit, raising a brow when she catches my eyes on her ass.

"Do you mind?"

I smirk and step closer to her, slowly running my finger over the edge of the thong at her hip. "Did you put this on for me?"

"No," she lies, avoiding my eyes while tossing her makeup into her fancy purse. "I need to go home now."

"Why?"

"Because I have homework to do," she lies again, turning away from me to grab her jeans from the side.

I snatch her wrist and spin her to face me, shoving her back against the wall beside the door. She grins and I take her waist with both hands, trapping her here with my hips pinned right up against hers.

We've gotten into a predictable pattern over the last couple weeks – I pretend she's my girlfriend and she pretends she's not, attempting to leave me every night like she belongs anywhere but here. I never let her go, but my stubborn girl still likes to fight me to save face.

"What are you doing?"

"I wanna make you all messy again," I inform her, tangling my fingers in her hair to pull her head back.

I lick the strawberry lip gloss from her mouth and feed her my gum, enjoying the way she takes what I give her without argument. I kiss her jaw and move my mouth down to her throat, groaning against her hot flesh when I get a taste of the shower gel lingering there.

She tastes like me and it's making me crazy.

I suck on her neck and she moans, rubbing her hot little pussy against the front of my sweats. "Xan."

"I know, baby," I say softly, dragging one of her thighs up to lock it around my hip. "Just a little one, okay? No one has to know."

She whimpers and I take that as a yes, gently digging my teeth into her skin to mark her as mine. Her hips buck and I remove my hand from her hair, sliding it down over her stomach to get to the waistband of her thong. I dip my fingers inside and find her clit with the middle one, teasing her and playing with her until she's writhing against me. As soon as I'm done with her neck, she pulls my mouth up to hers and sucks on my bottom lip, still rubbing on my dick through my sweats to set me off. It works and I squeeze her ass, pulling her away from the wall to back her up into my room. I push her down on the bed and fall down on top of her, shoving her legs apart to take my rightful spot between them. She grinds on me and I kiss her, fucking loving the way she lets herself go with me when no one's watching. Her phone rings on the nightstand and she ignores it, but then it rings again and she growls impatiently, ripping her mouth from mine to lean over and check it.

"Who is it?"

"Noah," she mutters, not noticing the way my jaw ticks because *why the fuck is that pretty boy bitch still calling my fucking girl?*

She reaches out to pick it up and I grab her wrist, taking the phone from her hand to stop her from hanging up on him. "I dare you to answer it."

She curses and I smirk like an asshole, hitting the green button to pass it back to her. She glares like she wants to kill me and lifts it up to her ear, her pastel blue eyes flashing with a mixture of panic and excitement.

"He–hello?" she stammers, shivering beneath me when I dip my head to lick the purple bruise on her neck.

Mine.

His muffled voice fills my ears and I run my hand over her inner thigh, spreading her out even further to get to her pussy. I lean up on one elbow beside her head and push her thong to the side, watching her face for her reaction while I slide two fingers inside her.

"Yeah, I uh.. I went out for a run," she tells him, her

eyes rolling at the pressure. "On the beach."

I steal the gum from her mouth and tease her clit with my thumb, laughing to myself when she bites down on her lip to cover the sounds creeping up her throat.

"Bad girl," I whisper in her ear, curling my knuckles to rub the spot that'll make her moan for me.

"Oh, shit- I mean no one," she rushes out, breathing hard against the side of my face. "I'm by m-myself."

I click my tongue at her lies and slide my fingers out of her pussy, slowly moving one down to tease her asshole with it. "Did you ever let him touch you here?"

She tenses but shakes her head, lifting her hips up off the bed to allow me better access. I work the tip inside and she whimpers before she can stop it, using her free hand to dig her nails into the back of my neck.

My little devil likes having one boy in each ear, me fingering her ass and making her shake while he listens on the other side.. it's making her reckless.

She pushes my head down and I give her what she wants, leaving a trail of open mouthed kisses on her stomach while I move to lie between her legs. She runs her hand through my hair and I lick her clit, grinning up at her when I hear him raise his voice through the phone.

"Sorry, I.. what did you say?"

He continues talking about fuck knows what and I continue eating her pussy, spitting on the finger in her ass to slide it in a little further. I get it up to the second knuckle and she cries out, quickly slapping a hand over her mouth in an attempt to keep it in. I playfully shake my head at her and squeeze her inner thigh with my free hand, increasing my pace on her clit to drive her wild. Her legs tremble like she's about to come and I groan without remorse, eagerly swallowing her down while she thrashes around like a fish out of water.

"JJ, what the *fuck* are you doing?!" Noah barks out, loud enough for me to hear every word.

"Get rid of him."

She does as she's told and tosses her phone to the side, quickly snatching both sides of my neck to yank me up to her mouth. "You're such an asshole."

"But you like it," I tease, pushing my sweats down to my thighs to pull my cock out. "You like being mine?"

She nods and I grin, rolling my hips out to run my piercing over her entrance. She lifts her ass up to get the tip in and I push my way inside, my head fucking spinning at the heat of her pussy surrounding me.

"Fuck, Xan," she moans into my mouth. "Do it again."

"Do what again?"

She pulls back to glare at me and I breathe a laugh, moving my hand down beneath her to get to her ass.

"I'm gonna put my dick in here someday," I inform her, dipping my head to slide my tongue over her bottom lip. "It's gonna feel so fucking good, baby. So fucking tight."

"Why can't you do it now?"

Fuck me.

"Because anal hurts if you don't do it right," I explain, slowing my pace to ensure I don't come before she does. "We need lube and you need more practice."

"I bet Trav's got lube."

"Probably, yeah," I agree. "You want me to go ask him

real quick?"

She opens her mouth to answer but snaps it shut again, frowning to herself while she thinks on that for a second. "Okay, I see your point."

I chuckle and circle her asshole with my middle finger, slipping it inside to stretch her out a little bit. I pull her up into me and she whimpers, grinding her hips on me to fuck me back hit for hit.

"Fuck, Jordyn," I grit out, leaning over her to drag her lip out between my teeth. "Rub your clit and feel how wet you are for me."

She reaches down between us and does as she's told, her mouth parting while she plays with herself. She tips her head back and I take full advantage, sliding my tongue between her lips to tease her with my piercing. She moans over and over again and fists my hair with her free hand, her pussy squeezing my cock in a fucking vice grip while she gets herself off.

"Goddamnit, baby, you're so fucking bad," I praise, knowing she's close. "Make yourself come."

"It's not *me*, Xan," she chokes out, her body shaking uncontrollably against mine. "*Fuck.*"

She comes and I ride us both through it, fucking her mouth with my tongue while my cock goes off inside her. She bites my lips and traps me between her thighs, pulling my hair so hard it hurts my scalp. I growl and slide my knees up to pin her beneath me, our heavy breathing mixing together while we attempt to come down from the high.

I'm so fucking high.

She's the best drug I've ever had and I'm officially addicted, out of control and desperate not to lose my fix.

A part of me feels like a piece of shit for stealing her because she's too good for me and I know it, but the other part of me doesn't give a fuck.

I accidentally stumbled upon the girl I want for life at eighteen years old and I'm fucking keeping her.

Indefinitely.

Bear whines at the patio door and I let out a sigh, leaving Jordyn curled up on my bed while I force myself up to pull my sweats back on. "Your daddy owes me big for leaving your needy ass with me," I mutter, walking over to unlock the door for him.

My girl chuckles behind me and I wink at her, following him outside to check what he's so worked up about. He walks over to the heated pool and I search the darkness, pulling my brows in when I find Travis sitting on the edge with his knees pulled up to his chest, a beer in his hands with his head hung low. Bear lies down on the concrete next to him and he looks up, rolling his eyes when he sees me standing beside him.

"You alright?"

He laughs lightly at that, but I don't think he finds me funny. "What are you doing, Xan?"

"What?"

"You know what," he slurs, flicking his wrist at the pool house behind me. "I didn't need Kian to tell me about you and her. You two have been sneakin' around out here for weeks, probably longer."

"Is that a problem for you?" I ask, dropping down on

his other side when he decides to remain silent. "Why are you so against me and her?"

"Because she's supposed to be Noah's," he says bluntly, lifting his beer to his mouth to swallow it down. "He thinks she's sitting at home by herself every night to fix her broken pride, taking a minute to cool off before she eventually takes him back."

I highly doubt it considering what he heard on the phone earlier tonight, but I don't tell him that.

"If he finds out she's been fuckin' around with you this whole time, he's gonna retaliate."

"I don't give a shit what he does."

"I know you don't but *I* do," he stresses. "I actually care about that girl in your bed, you idiot."

"Fucking please, man, you don't even know her."

He frowns at that, pulling his head back to bounce his eyes between mine. "What the fuck does that mean?"

My jaw ticks but I keep my mouth shut, partly because I don't feel like arguing with him but mostly because it's not my place to tell her secrets.

He doesn't know that creepy horror movies make her hot or that she likes the marshmallows beneath the cream or that she's insecure about her body thanks to the endless amount of times people have tried to tear her down to their level. He doesn't know about the pictures or Washington or that this bullshit life she's been forced into is killing her slowly, day by fucking day.

He doesn't know her like I do.

No one does.

He raises a cocky ass brow and I chuckle, pulling my

cigarettes out of my pocket to light one up. "I like her, Trav," I admit. "I *really* fucking like her."

"Maybe that's true but what happens when you get bored in a week or a month or a year from now?" he asks, lowering his voice to ensure she won't hear what comes next. "You're gonna break her heart, man."

"No, I'm not," I say simply, looking over my shoulder to watch her through the window. "I'm not that guy anymore."

"Since when?"

I shrug and blow my smoke out, grinning to myself while I give him the only answer there is. "Since her."

Little Devil

23

Jordyn

He takes this game way too seriously.

It doesn't matter what I dare him to do, I can't get him to say no to me. I've made him drink a glass of hot sauce, made him wear my underwear for an entire day, I've even painted his nails, for fuck's sake, and yet here he stands, staring at me from across the hall with his back resting on his locker and his phone in his hand, his black nails on full display for all to see.

I need to up my game.

So that's exactly what I've done.

Xander: You can't be serious.

Jordyn: I'm so serious.

Xander: That's cheating.

Jordyn: Baby, that's winning.

He shakes his head at me and I smirk, knowing I've

got him this time, but then he shocks the shit out of me and removes his crooked tie from his neck, tossing it into his locker over his shoulder.

He wouldn't..

"What's he doing?" Kian asks from beside me, dropping his jaw when Xan removes his shirt from his body and gets to work on the zipper of his pants. "Oh my *god.*"

I lift my hands to cover my mouth and the hall erupts into chaos, most of the girls squealing and staring at *my* goddamn man while he strips his clothes, not stopping until he's butt ass naked in front of at least half of the entire senior class. Sienna drags her lip out through her teeth and I scrub my hands over my cheeks, inwardly cursing myself for coming up with such a stupid dare.

This was a bad idea.

He cocks his head like he heard me and I drop my eyes to his dick, not missing the way he can barely keep it covered with one hand. Kian stares at his form with a shameless grin on his face and Travis lets out an aggravated breath, pinching the bridge of his nose with a look that screams *fucking idiot.*

"Dude, my mom's comin–"

"Alexander Reid!" the principal screeches, making several students *and* staff members jump while she makes her way through the parted crowd to get to us.

"Yes, ma'am?" he asks, still staring at me.

"*Alexander*," I mouth, making him laugh.

"For goodness sake, just.. cover yourself up and go to my office," she grits out, her face burning with a mixture of embarrassment and rage. "*Now!*"

Oh, fuck.

Forty seven minutes later, my phone buzzes with a text and I take it out to check it, only releasing the breath I was holding when I realize his aunt hasn't killed him yet.

Xander: Tell him you need to go to the bathroom.

Xander: Bring your shit with you.

I pull my brows in at that, hesitating a minute before I decide to do as I'm told. A few students follow me with their eyes but I ignore them, my heels tapping along the floor while I walk over to the teacher's desk.

"Can I go to the bathroom, please?"

He waves his permission without looking up and I slip out into the hall, squealing when two hands snatch my waist from behind.

"Xan," I hiss, laughing when he smacks my ass and spins me to face him. "What happened?"

"I got suspended."

"And you're happy about that?"

"Baby, I've got three days off," he teases, leaning over me to link our fingers together. "You wanna skip last period with me?"

I chew my lip and drop my eyes to our hands, smiling to myself at the sight of the black nail polish on my fingernails. I'm not supposed to wear this cheap crap, as my mother calls it, but he wanted to paint mine after I finished his and I let him do it, mostly for the game but also because I've become a love sick fool with no brain.

"Can I drive?" I ask, backing away from him to head towards the exit at the end of the hall.

He tosses me his keys and I clap my hands like a five year old, leading the way to the parking lot to jump into the drivers seat of his badass Camaro.

"Do you know what pussy whipped means?" he asks, sliding in beside me to toss our bags into the back.

"Yeah, why?"

"No reason," he mutters, taking his phone out to connect it to the stereo. "Where'd you wanna go?"

I shrug and reach back to find my own keys, lifting them up to show him the purple devil key chain he gave me all those weeks ago. "Wanna know a secret?"

24

Xander

She looks nervous.

And excited.

Then right back to nervous while she leads me along past her bedroom, stopping to face me fully when we get to a set of double doors at the end of the hall. "This is stupid," she decides. "Maybe we should just go start a fire or something instea–"

I shake my head at her and take her face in my hands, laughing lightly when I realize she'd rather commit arson with me than show me what's in there.

"Baby."

"What?" she asks, bouncing her eyes between mine.

"Will you open it now?"

She takes a breath and shoves the key into the lock, side eyeing me over her shoulder while I follow her inside. She closes the door behind us and I look around, frowning when I find nothing but blackness.

What..?

"This used to be my dad's office," she says from somewhere beside me, flicking a switch on the wall to bathe the room in a dark red glow. "My mom didn't want it for anything so.. it's mine now."

I blink and wait for my eyes to adjust, grinning when I spot the several pictures pegged up on the three lines hanging above us. The windows are completely blacked out and she's got three long tables set up in neat rows, the surfaces filled with bottles of liquid and film cassettes and other materials I can't name.

"Is this a dark room?"

She nods and tucks her hair behind her ears, smiling to herself when she catches the excitement on my face. I like it when she opens up with me like this, when she shows me things she's never shown anyone before. It makes me fucking giddy to know she trusts me over them, to know she *chooses* me over them.

It makes me hers.

"I like this one," I tell her, carefully hovering my finger below the picture of us kissing on the beach that night, unsure if I'm allowed to touch.

"You mean the only one I *didn't* take?" she jokes, making me laugh.

Seemingly more content than she was a minute ago, she washes her hands at the sink in the corner and then walks back over to me, reaching up to remove the photo from the line.

"They're dry now?" I ask, and she nods, tossing the pegs into the box on the side while she moves along to do the same with the rest.

She tries to explain the whole process to me and I do my best to keep up with her, but I honestly don't have a fucking clue what she's talking about. She chuckles like she knows it and removes the last one from its peg, tilting her head at me to follow her to the two seater couch on the back wall. I drop my ass down and she sits back between my legs, comfortably resting her head on my shoulder while she goes through the photos one by one. She lifts her knees up to her chest and I wrap my arms around her waist, enjoying the way her body molds against mine like it was made for me.

"Where's your dad, Jordyn?" I ask after a while, gently running my thumb over her waist beneath her shirt. "You never talk about him."

"That's because there's not much to talk about," she says quietly. "I don't know where he is."

"What do you mean?"

"He left my mom and married another man when I was five," she explains, but she doesn't seem mad or bitter about it. "I haven't seen or heard from him since."

My brows dip and I tighten my arms around her waist, leaning over her to kiss the spot beneath her ear. "It's his loss, baby."

"I know," she whispers, turning her head to smile at me.

She reaches up to pull my tie over her shoulder and I watch her run her fingers over it, unable to stop myself from wanting more. "What's your biggest secret?"

"You are," she answers, mindlessly threading her tie through mine to knot them together. "*You're* my secret."

"Yeah?" I tease, moving my hands up to squeeze her

ribs. "What's your favorite thing about me?"

"Your abs," she deadpans. "Definitely your abs."

I laugh and she moves the photos from her lap to the couch next to us, quiet a minute before she speaks again.

"It's your take on life," she admits, still playing with our knotted ties. "The way you're just *you* without apologizing for it. The way you put yourself first and take what you want. The way you have *fun*. I wish I had the balls to be more like you."

I smile to myself and lift her chin up with my forefinger, leaning into her to speak over her lips. "It's okay to be who you are, baby."

"I know but.. what if no one likes who I am?"

"It doesn't matter," I say simply. "All that matters is that you like yourself."

Silence follows and I'm just about to tell her how fucking pretty she is, but then she turns around and covers my mouth with her hand. "My turn to ask the questions," she decides, spreading her legs out to straddle my thighs. "What's *your* biggest secret?"

I smirk at that, grinding my cock up against her pussy while I sort through all the shitty things I've done over the years. "I had a threesome with my teacher and her stepson a few months ago."

Her eyes widen and her mouth parts, her cheeks glowing even brighter than usual thanks to the red lights surrounding us. "Was she married to his dad?"

"Yep."

"Do you regret it?"

"Not really."

"What *do* you regret, then?" she asks, resting her forearms on my shoulders, raking her fingers through my hair. "What's your biggest mistake, Xan?"

That one hits me where it hurts and I clear my throat, hesitating a second while I consider how to put this. "I uh.. I got my brother killed."

Her face falls and she pinches her eyebrows together, her eyes filling with tears when she catches the look in mine. "Xan.."

"He wasn't mad about it," I whisper, laughing lightly at the memory of the last words he ever spoke to me. "The stupid fucker found it kind of funny, actually.."

Little Devil

25

three years ago

Xander

"Nik, come on," I complain, dropping down on the edge of his bed to shake him. "You promised you'd take me out."

"Fuck off, you little shit," he mumbles, speaking into his pillow. "I'm sleeping."

"You've been asleep all day."

"Yeah, because I was awake all night," he throws back, whipping his arm out to shove me down on my ass.

I sigh and pull myself up to stand, smirking when I connect eyes with the naked brunette girl spread out beside him. I wink at her and she winks back, rolling over onto her side to lift her thigh over my brother's waist.

"Hey, Nik?" I ask, raising a brow at her when she reaches down to wrap her fist around his cock.

"What, Xan?"

"I dare you."

He growls and throws the covers away, covering his dick with his hand while he jumps up to point a finger at my face. "If Mom finds out about this, I'm throwin' your sorry ass under the bus."

I grin and he flips me off, walking away to lock himself in the bathroom. His date looks at me and I step closer to her, but then the bathroom door opens again and he leans over to snatch her hand, pulling her up to take her with him. Her knees hit the floor and I let out a snort, leaving his bedroom to go wait for him in mine.

Selfish bastard.

A little over three hours later, I'm wasted on a mixture of I don't know what and Nik's got some random blonde girl on his lap, smirking at me over her shoulder while she sucks his neck on the upper level of the club he brought me to. His dark brown hair falls over his eyes the same way mine does and she pushes it back for him, wrapping her arms around his neck to grind on his dick through his jeans. I shake my head with a smile and take my drinks from the bartender, turning around to go back to my brother and the rest of our friends, but then a shoulder bumps mine and I whip my head around, accidentally spilling a little vodka on her arm.

"Shit, I'm sorry," I shout over the music, blinking when I realize it's the same girl I saw in Nik's bed earlier tonight. "Hey."

"Hey," she mutters, quickly cutting her eyes left and right like she's afraid of something.

She's got black streaks of makeup running down her

cheeks and her red lipstick is smeared all over her mouth, her neck and wrists covered in bruises that definitely weren't there when she left my house a few hours ago.

"Are you alrigh–"

"Gen!" a male voice barks from behind her, roughly snatching her arm to pull her into him. "How many times do I have to tell you to stop running away from me?"

She swallows and backs away from him, her eyes wide with genuine fear like he's about to fucking hit her. He takes a threatening step forward and I set my drinks down on the bar, instinctively moving between them to block his path. He keeps on coming and I shove his ass back, not missing the creepy tick in his jaw or the rage in his eyes, his nostrils split and cracked from the amount of coke he's sucked up through his nose.

"Get the fuck away from her."

"Who the fuck is this kid?" he asks at the same time, craning his neck to look at her. "Is this him?"

She shakes her head no and he wraps his hands around my neck, roughly digging his thumbs into my throat to choke me. I pull back a bit to punch him in the nose and he stumbles back a step, angrily spitting the blood from his mouth before he comes right back for more. I'm just about to hit him again, but then he's yanked away from me by his shirt and I'm surrounded on all sides.

"That's my fucking brother, you stupid piece of shit," Nik bites out, shoving him down on his ass to bang his head against the floor.

Shouts and screams fill my ears and our little corner of the club erupts into uncontrollable chaos – his boys fighting with ours while my big brother beats the shit out of Gen's ex-boyfriend, I'm assuming.

Little Devil

"The one night we bring you out, little Reid," our friend Justin teases, playfully shaking his head at me while he steals my drink from the bar.

I laugh and search the crowd for Nik, not finding him at first, but then I do and my heart leaps up into my throat, my eyes dropping to the broken glass bottle sticking out of his stomach.

"Nik!" I shout, rushing him in the same breath, but I don't get to him in time before the guy who just stabbed my fucking brother rips the glass out of his flesh and pushes him back, sending him flying over the railing and down towards the dance floor below us.

No.

Please, no.

More hysterical screams echo throughout the club and I'm running as fast as I can, jumping over the staircase to drop to my knees beside him. He's still awake, lying on his back with his legs tangled up beneath him, a sickening amount of blood pouring from his stomach as well as the fresh wound on his temple. I panic and rip my t-shirt over my head, pressing that to his temple while I press my bare hand to his abdomen. One of the bartenders drops down beside me and hands me a couple hand towels to use instead, her phone pressed to her ear while she rattles off words and phrases that make me want to throw up.

Stabbed.

Bleeding out.

Fucking paralyzed.

This can't be real.

His hazel eyes seek mine and he frowns, almost like he doesn't realize what's happening yet. "Xan."

"Nik," I choke out, barely recognizing the sound of my own voice. "Goddamnit."

"It's bad, isn't it?"

"*No*," I growl, frantically shaking my head to reassure us both. "No, it's fine. You're gonna be fine."

He laughs at that, because of course my idiot brother would laugh at a time like this. "You suck at lying."

Fucking hell.

Thick tears stream over my face and he smiles at me, slowly lifting his hand up to the back of my neck to pull me into him. "Do me a favor, okay?"

"What favor?" I ask, trying and failing to hide the sob creeping up my throat.

"Don't let this change you into something you're not," he croaks out, sucking a shaky breath into his lungs before he continues. "I don't want you becoming a moody little bitch with no friends and no life."

"What am I supposed to be?"

"Just be *you*," he says simply. "Irresponsible and reckless and fuckin' stupid, like always."

I shake my head and he tries to tighten his grip on me, weakly squeezing my jaw to pull my eyes back to his pale ones.

They're fading.

He's dying right in front of me and I can't stop it.

"Promise me, Xan."

"And if I don't?"

"I'll haunt your skinny ass until you cry," he jokes,

smirking when he catches the look on my face.

"You're not funny."

"I think I'm funny."

I cry and rest my forehead against his, hugging him the best I can with my hands where they are.

"Hey, Xan?"

"What?" I ask through my tears, pulling back an inch to look him in the eye.

"I dare you."

26

present

Jordyn

My heart hurts for him and I bury my face into the crook of his neck, gently running my nails over his scalp in an attempt to comfort him. "It wasn't your fault, Xan," I whisper, barely managing to hide the silent tears leaking from my eyes. "You were just a kid. You didn't know what would happen."

He chuckles sadly at that, tightening his arms around my waist while he kisses the side of my head. "My parents don't agree with you, princess. They know I started the fight with the guy who killed him. They think it should have been me."

"They said that to you?"

He shrugs and I close my eyes, pissed off and disgusted at the way they've treated their own son for the last three years. I get they must have been heartbroken after Niko died, I really do, but if I ever have children of my own someday, I like to think I'd love them unconditionally – something we've both missed out on, it seems.

"Do you want kids?" I blurt out, immediately kicking myself for asking him that.

Nice work, idiot.

"Yeah," he answers, not even a little bit put out by my stupidity. "Two boys and a girl. I want us to have the boys first, though, so they can protect her when they're older. Me and Nik always wanted a little sister."

I blink at that, slowly pulling back to look at him. "That was a joke, right?"

"No. We wanted to call her Frankie."

I roll my lips and he smirks at me, clearly waiting for me to call him out for what he said just now – *us*, like it's inevitable – but I don't do that. Instead I run my hands over his neck and down to the chain there, carefully pulling it out to lie it down over his shirt.

"Was this his?" I ask, brushing my finger over the silver cross on his chest. "Is that why you never take it off?"

He nods and I lift my eyes back to his, pulling my brows in when I catch the stupid grin on his face. I'm just about to ask him why he's looking at me like that considering we're talking about his dead brother, but then our phones go off with a string of messages and I shut my mouth. I pull mine out to check it and he does the same, both of us looking down to open the three way group chat Kian added us to just now.

Kian: You two bitches better not miss my party.

Kian: I'm making margaritas.

Kian: Everyone knows you left together, by the way.

Kian: Noah looks like he wants to kill someone.

Kian: It's hilarious.

Xan laughs and I shake my head at him, setting my phone down on the couch to take his face in my hands. "You wanna go with me?"

"Will you ride my dick first?" he asks, sliding his hands over my thighs beneath my skirt.

I nod a little faster than necessary and he pulls my thong to the side, reaching down between us to take his cock out of his pants. He spits on his fingers to wet my pussy and I sink down on him, moaning at the feel of his piercing inside me. I tip my head back and roll my hips out, riding him just like he told me to.

"Fuck, baby," he whispers, wrapping our still knotted ties around his fist to pull me into him. "You're so fucking sexy."

My pussy throbs at the look in his eyes and I kiss him, sucking on his lips and his tongue while he gets me off with his free hand. I fumble with the buttons on my shirt and shove it down to my shoulders, raking my fingers through his hair to pull his mouth to my neck. He chuckles like an asshole but gives me what I want all the same, still rubbing my clit with his thumb while he teases my pulse with his lips.

I like having his mark on me and he knows it.

My very own dirty little secret.

"Do it," I plead, ignoring how desperate and needy it makes me sound. "Now, Xan."

He sinks his teeth into my flesh and I moan loudly, roughly digging my nails into his neck to keep him there. My orgasm hits me like a tidal wave and I grind on him to make it last as long as possible, fucking loving the way he groans against me with his own release. His cum leaks out of my pussy and he squeezes my ass, leaning back a bit to look down between us.

"So fucking sexy," he repeats, pulling his dick out to slide the tip over my clit. "I wanna go again."

"Already?"

He nods, pulling me in to press his lips to my ear. "You gonna let me fuck you up against the wall in your rich girl shower?"

"Fuck, yes."

Kian's jaw drops to the floor when he sees me and Travis chokes on his beer, his eyes damn near bugging out of his head while he stares at me and my form. I'm wearing a black bralette with a pair of ripped jeans over some high waisted fishnet tights, my hair tied up into a straight, messy ponytail at the top of my head.

"Not for you, asshole," Xan says from beside me, playfully shoving his cousin's head away before he leans over to kiss my neck. "You want a drink?"

I nod and he winks at me, backing away to walk over to the bar set up on Kian's kitchen island. The boys continue to stare and I chew the inside of my cheek, feeling a little self conscious when I realize they're not the only ones looking at me like I've grown two heads.

"I, uh.." I trail off, awkwardly clearing my throat while I decide what to say to them. "Xan helped me get dressed, okay?"

"Yeah, we can see that," Kian chuckles, taking my hands to pull me into him. "Baby, you look *fine*. I kinda hate you for it, though."

"What? Why?"

"Because my *fuck buddy* looks like he wants your ass more than he wants mine," he jokes, but I don't miss the clear dig intended for the boy behind him.

"Ki," Travis grits out, but Kian just flips him off and pulls me away, keeping hold of my hand while we make our way through the parted crowd.

"What was that about?"

"Nothing," he says lamely, but I'm not buying it.

"Kian."

"JJ," he mocks my tone, rolling his eyes when he catches the look on my face. "What?"

"Sweetie, he's more than just a fuck buddy."

"Try telling him that," he mutters. "He doesn't want me for anything *more* than an easy la–"

"The fuck I don't," Travis cuts in, snatching his neck to pull his back to his chest.

Kian yelps and I run my thumb over my lips, doing my best to hide my laugh while Travis drags him away from me. They disappear around the corner and I move to go find Xan, sighing when I come face to face with my ex-boyfriend. I've gotten really good at avoiding him over the last few weeks, even more so since the night I talked to him on the phone while Xan made me come for him to hear it, but it seems my luck just ran out.

"What do you want?"

"What the fuck are you wearing?" he bites back, curling his lip in disgust while he moves his eyes from my face to my heels and back up again.

A bitter laugh leaves me and I cock my head at him, honest to god wondering what I ever saw in this narcissistic piece of shit. I was sure I was in love with him when we were kids, but lately I've been starting to wonder if that's only because I'd have done anything to make my mother happy. She wanted me to love Noah so I did it, convinced myself that was what love felt like and rolled with it because I had to.

It wasn't love, though, was it?

I get that now.

His nostrils flare like he knows it and he opens his mouth to say something else, but then Xan shoves his ass to the side and takes his place in front of me, casually handing me a margarita like the last three seconds didn't happen. I raise a brow and he takes my hand in his, pulling me into him to speak over my lips.

"*Mine.*"

I hide a grin and he grins back, ignoring Noah completely while he leads me out towards the makeshift dance floor by the pool. I wrap my arm around his neck and lift my drink to my lips, enjoying the way he dances with me without a care in the world. He spins me around and I grin for real this time, but my mood soon changes when I catch Sienna staring at us from her spot in the kitchen. This isn't the first time I've caught her looking and it probably won't be the last, and even though I know Xan would *probably* never go there, I can't deny the anxiety running through me at the thought of him cheating on me with her.

Or anyone.

"What's on your mind, princess?" he asks me, gently tipping my chin up to pull my eyes back to his.

"Sienna wants to fuck you," I say childishly, huffing out an annoyed breath when I catch the amusement on his face.

"You think that's funny?"

"I think you're jealous," he teases, dipping his head to drag my bottom lip out through his teeth. "And even though it makes my dick really fucking hard, you have *no* fucking reason to be. I want *you*, Jordyn James. Even when you're not looking, *you're* all I want."

"Is that right?" I draw out, struggling to hide the way my heart skips *all* the damn beats. "And if I dared you to kiss another girl?"

"I'd lose the game," he says simply, shrugging like he didn't just lie to my face.

"No, you wouldn't."

"Dare me, then," he challenges, wrapping both arms around my waist to rest his forehead on mine. "You wanna win, right? Dare me to go kiss someone else and I'll fucking *show* you how much you mean to me."

I blink at that, momentarily shocked into silence because *fuck me*, he's serious.

He waits like he thinks I'll do it but I shake my head, holding his eyes while I set my drink down on the pool table beside us. "Kiss me instead."

"You sure?" he asks. "Right here in front of all your judgy little friends?"

I smirk and slide my hands up to his neck, pulling him down to run my fingers through his hair. "I dare you."

He presses his lips to mine and I kiss him back, ignoring the whispers and the several pairs of eyes on us while I seek out his piercing with my tongue.

They don't fucking get it and they probably never will, but I don't care anymore.

I want him and I'm taking him, just like he taught me to.

"Xan," I whisper, hesitating a second before I decide to tell him. "I think I'm falling for you."

A light laugh leaves him and he smiles against my lips, still moving with me to the beat of the music. "Baby, I've already fallen."

27

Xander

"I love your skin," she tells me, gently running her nails over the ink on my forearms. "It's so pretty."

"*Pretty*?" I ask, amused by her and her inability to tolerate alcohol.

I've never seen her finish a single drink in the two months I've known her. She usually takes one sip of whatever she's given and sets it down somewhere, but tonight she swallowed two margaritas and four purple jello shots one after the other. I cut her off about an hour ago once we got back to Travis' house with him and Kian, but that hasn't stopped her from stealing sips of my beer when she thinks I'm not looking.

I think my girl likes being tipsy.

"I look so bare next to you," she goes on, sticking her lip out with a cute ass pout that makes me want to bite it.

She's wearing nothing but a tiny little black thong, lying back on my chest with her ass on my dick and her legs spread out over mine, the bubbles from the hot tub effectively hiding her nipples from the two boys opposite. I'm not worried about Kian considering pussy's not his thing, but I won't hesitate to make my cousin's nose bleed if I catch him looking at what's mine. The asshole smirks like he knows it and I flip him off, ignoring his chuckle while I dip my head to kiss her neck. She moans quietly and I slide my hands over her stomach, enjoying the way her warm skin feels against mine beneath the water.

"Will you give me a tattoo?" she asks out of nowhere, tipping her head back on my shoulder to look at me.

I raise a brow at that, hiding a laugh when I catch the disgust slash horror on Travis' face.

"Don't even–"

"Fuck, yeah," Kian says excitedly, earning himself a sideways glare from his boyfriend.

"You're all idiots," he informs us, averting his eyes when Jordyn stands up and snatches my hand to take me with her. "For fuck's sake, Xan, she's drunk."

"She's not *drunk*," I argue, grabbing a towel from the side to wrap it around her body. "She's just happy."

He sighs angrily and she grins, looking up at me with a heated stare that makes me ache while she leads us back to the pool house. I set my beer down on the nightstand and lie her down on my bed, leaving her there a minute while I grab the black case from the bottom of my closet. I take one of my shirts out and slide it on over her head, pulling it down to her thighs to ensure they can't see her through the windows.

"What do you want, baby?"

"I want a surprise," she answers, lazily folding her arm

beneath her head to bare her body for me.

I groan and adjust my dick in my boxers, sitting down beside her to run my thumb over the inner corner of her wrist beneath her little finger. "Right here, okay?"

She nods and I lean over her to kiss her lips, teasing her tongue with my piercing while I wait for her to change her mind. She doesn't, though, so I pull back and snap my gloves on, watching her closely while I use a little rubbing alcohol to clean her up.

"Will it hurt?" she asks, frowning at me when I take a razor to run it over her skin.

"A little bit, yeah, but it won't take long."

"What are you doing?"

"Shaving you," I say simply, laughing lightly when she scrunches her nose in confusion. "Relax, princess, it's just a couple baby hairs."

She sinks back into the pillows and I busy myself getting ready, pausing to look up at her with the needle hovering over her pure, untouched flesh. She nods eagerly and I get to work, enjoying the consistent buzz of the gun in my ears while I mark her with my ink.

"Ow, you fucker!" she bites out, digging her black nails into her palm while she struggles to keep still. "That hurts more than a *little* bit, Xan. Jesus, fuck."

I chuckle and wipe the blood away, gently running my thumb over the four half moon shaped indents on the inside of her hand. "You want me to stop?"

She winces but shakes her head, taking a long breath to ready herself. "No, it's okay. Keep going."

I smile to myself and dip my head to do as I'm told, holding her wrist steady with my free hand while I do the only thing I'm good at. She winces again when I get to the shading and covers her face with her forearm, her toes curling into the mattress beside me. Other than that, though, she doesn't make a sound, which is pretty damn impressive considering this is one of the most painful places to get a tattoo.

"Good girl," I praise, wiping it down again before I finish the last part. "Okay, baby, you're done."

She releases the breath she's been holding and lifts her head to look at it, biting down on her bottom lip to hide that sexy little grin on her face. I'll give her something bigger when she's sober if that's what she really wants, but for now I've kept it small and simple – a blacked out, faceless version of the purple devil emoji.

"You like it?"

She nods and sits up to take my face in her hands, moving towards me on her knees to pull my mouth up to hers. "How good are you at tattooing yourself?"

I smirk at that, squeezing her bare ass to pull her into me. She sits down on the edge of the bed beside me and I switch my needle out for a clean one, quickly prepping my skin the same way I did hers just now. I start on my outline and hold her wrist out next to mine, bouncing my eyes between the two to ensure they match in size. As soon as I get done with it, she grins like a kid in a candy shop and grabs her camera from her purse, linking our little fingers together while she snaps a picture of them side by side.

"Are you gonna hate me for this in the morning?" I ask, tipping her chin up to search her eyes.

"Maybe a little bit," she teases, gently pulling on my

lips with her teeth. "Can I have some more beer now?"

    I laugh and snatch her waist to lie her down across my lap, taking my drink from the nightstand to pass it to her. "You can have whatever the fuck you want, baby girl."

Little Devil

28

Jordyn

I wake up the next morning with a headache from hell and a wrap on my left wrist, my eyelids sticking together while I lift my head to look around.

"Xan?" I croak out, frowning to myself when I realize the light flooding through the windows is physically painful to look at.

I'm never drinking again.

His quiet laugh rings out from somewhere beside me and I look up, smiling like an idiot when I find him sitting down on the edge of the bed with a coffee in one hand and two white pills in the other. I take the pills without asking what they are and swallow them down, sitting up against the headboard to sip my coffee.

"Where did you go?"

"I had to feed Bear and take him out for a walk," he explains, lying down on his front between my legs to rest his chin on my stomach.

"Already?" I ask, a little offended he didn't ask me to go with him. "What time is it?"

"Almost ten thirty."

"What? Why didn't you wake me up yet?"

"I tried," he chuckles. "You shoved my head away and said *no, asshole, my fucking brain hurts.*"

I roll my lips to hide a grin and he lifts my shirt up to my waist, dipping his head to kiss his way from my navel to my hip bone. My body feels like shit but I still revel in the attention, lazily running my fingers through his hair to keep him there.

"Travis and Kian are going for breakfast at Lucky's in a minute," he tells me. "You wanna go?"

I moan my agreement and lift my mug to my lips, turning my wrist over to show him the ink there. "Can I get this wet yet? I need to take a shower."

"Yeah, just don't put it directly under the water and try not to get too much soap on it."

I nod and he takes the wrap off for me, standing up to toss it into the trash can beside the bed. I sulk like a child at the loss of his skin on mine and he smirks at me, leaning over to speak over my lips.

"Go get your body nice and wet for me and I'll sneak inside and lick your pussy," he whispers, taking the coffee from my hands to set it down on the nightstand.

My eyes darken with need and I force myself up to do as I'm told, laughing lightly when he snatches my waist from behind and follows me into the bathroom.

Despite what he just said, there is no *sneaking*.

The horny bastard stays on my ass all the way to the

shower head.

"How much do you like this hoodie?" I ask, falling back in my seat to gesture to said hoodie.

He frowns at that, bouncing his eyes between me and the road in confusion. "I don't know. I mean, I like it a lot better on you than me. Why?"

"Because if you don't stop driving like an asshole, I'm gonna throw up all over it," I warn, scrubbing my hands over my face in an attempt to ease the sickness.

He laughs at me and pulls up next to Travis' car outside the diner we're meeting them at. I damn near fall out of the passenger side and he comes around to get me, still laughing while he takes my hand to lead me through the parking lot. It's overflowing inside considering it's lunch time on a Sunday, but I already know the boys'll be sitting in our regular booth at the back just like they are every weekend. Xan opens the main door for me and I follow him in, gratefully taking the sunglasses he passes me to shove them on over my eyes.

"This is the worse feeling ever," I mutter, leaning into his side with his arm wrapped around my neck.

"You'll be fine once you get some food in you," he assures me, sweetly kissing my temple while we make our way to the back of the line next to the counter. "You know what you want yet?"

"A big stack of pancakes and an iced coffee with–"

"A shit load of syrup," he finishes for me, lifting my chin up to press his lips to mine. "Go sit down and I'll bring your coffee over when it's done, okay?"

"Okay, boyfriend," I say dryly, struggling to hide the smile on my face while I move to do as I'm told.

He smacks my ass and I let out a squeal, ignoring the looks thrown my way while I walk through the crowd towards the eight seater booth at the back of the diner. I find Travis and Kian sitting right where I knew they'd be, but my step falters when I spot Noah sitting across from them with Penelope and Sienna either side of him.

"..really just gonna sit here and ignore the fact that she's like.. *together* with the new boy now?" Penelope asks, clearly not noticing me standing a few feet away.

"What's wrong with that?" Kian shrugs, reaching over to steal a sip of Travis' coffee.

"It's weird," she tells the group, scrunching her nose up in disgust. "*He's* weird."

"I think he's hot," Sienna adds helpfully, and I nod my head, casually shoving my hands into the pocket of Xan's hoodie while I wait for one of them to notice me.

"That's because you're an idiot," Penelope bites back, folding her arms across her chest while she leans back on Noah's outstretched arm.

Sienna shrugs it off and takes her compact mirror out of her purse, quickly checking her hair and make up before she speaks again. "Isn't it funny how Travis dared him to fuck her and she ended up falling for him? I mean, how gullible do you have to be?"

"The fuck are you talkin' about, Si?" Travis frowns. "I didn't dare him to do shit."

"Yes, you did," she argues, chuckling to herself at the memory. "I heard you two talking that night at her birthday party when he first got here."

He sighs like he's been caught and I pull my head back, swallowing the embarrassment creeping up my throat while I glance between them and Xan. Noah chooses that exact moment to look up and I force my features even, but of course I'm not fast enough. He cocks his head at me and I fist my hands inside my pocket, barely resisting the urge to smack that stupid grin off his face. Travis catches him looking at something over his shoulder and follows his line of sight, his face falling when he realizes I'm standing right beside him.

"Oh, shit."

"Fuck you, Trav."

"JJ, wait, it wasn't like that," he tries, but I'm already gone, shaking my head at him and myself while I slip through the crowd and out to the parking lot.

I toss the asshole's sunglasses onto the hood of his car but keep the hoodie, protectively folding my arms around my body while I walk away. Not wanting one of my mother's drivers to see me looking like this, I jump into a yellow cab and ask the driver to take me to the beach near my house, thankful I grabbed my purse before we left the pool house earlier. My phone rings against my thigh but I ignore it, cursing myself when I feel the silent tears leaking from my eyes.

"Stop crying," I whisper. "Stop it, stop it, stop it."

The cab driver looks at me funny and I force a smile, quickly wiping my cheeks with my sleeves before I take my wallet out to pay him. I'm not sure how much to tip him for a five minute ride, so I give him a hundred dollars and mutter a quiet thank you, jumping out to head down to the small coffee shop on the beach. I buy my own damn iced coffee with extra syrup and sip it while I walk, struggling to think about anything but him and the way he's made me feel for the last two months.

Like someone finally wanted me for *me*.

Like I actually meant more to him than this stupid game he plays so well.

So fucking stupid.

My phone continues to ring and I turn it off, looking up when I find a hot guy playing football with a few others on the sand by the water. He's shirtless and tanned with muscles in all the right places, his dark hair falling over his forehead in a way that reminds me of Xan. He catches me looking and smirks at me, slowly walking over with his ball in his hands and his eyes on my form.

"Hey."

"Hey," I say back, purposely giving him the same once over he gave me. "Can I take your picture?"

29

Xander

I slam my car door closed and then punch it for good measure, nervously running my hands through my hair while I walk across the parking lot to meet Travis and Kian. I drove to the city right after she ran away from me and searched the entire fucking beach, thinking that's where she'd have gone to cool off and take a few strangers' pictures, but I didn't think to check the beach two miles from her fucking house.

Fuck me, this girl's got me in knots.

"Where is she?"

Travis tilts his head towards the party and I follow them, grinding my teeth when I find some black haired asshole talking to *my* fucking girlfriend on the sand next to the bonfire. She's been hiding from me all goddamn day, and the relief of finally finding her mixed with the anger of catching her with some random guy she doesn't know has my head fucking spinning.

I should kick his ass just for looking at her.

Little Devil

Just as I think it, she looks around over her shoulder and her eyes hit mine, her jaw working overtime while she lifts a red solo cup to her mouth. Her feet are bare and she's wearing my hoodie like an oversized dress, her sleeves bunched up to her elbows and her tanned thighs on full display for all to see. She says something that makes him laugh and I laugh, too, quickly stealing Travis' drink from his hand to swallow it down.

"Xan.." he warns, somehow knowing I'm about two and a half feet away from losing my shit because if that prick takes one more fucking step..

"The fuck is *he* doing here?" Noah barks out, his nostrils flaring when I flick the empty cup at his face.

"Hey, Xan," Sienna says from beside Penelope, biting her lip while she twirls her blonde hair around her finger, but I'm already walking away because *fuck her*.

"Beat it," I tell the guy next to my girl, shoving his ass back when he refuses to move.

"*Xan*," Jordyn snaps, dropping her jaw while she looks from me to him and back again.

"Dude, what the fu–"

"I said beat it," I repeat, not even bothering to look his way while I snatch Jordyn's waist to pull her into me.

She lets out a surprised scream and I lock my arm around her back, ignoring the way she smacks my chest and struggles against my hold because it's pointless.

"Get off m–"

"Nah, I'm not playing this game with you, baby girl." I inform her, grabbing her jaw with my free hand to lift her eyes up to mine. "You listen to me and you listen good because I'm only gonna say this once. Whatever you heard today was just some bullshit line I came out with the first time I saw you. I don't care what that bitch says. He never dared me to fuck you. No one did."

"That's not the point, Xan," she whisper yells, knocking my hand from her face, then gesturing to the large group of people watching our every move. "Everyone thinks the only reason you chased me so hard back then was to win a fucking game. They think it was all fake."

"Who gives a fuck what they think?"

"That's easy for you to say when you're the big man and I'm the dumbass who fell for your shit," she bites back, loud enough for them to hear it this time.

Several brows jump at her little bad girl outburst and I pinch my lips together, slowly raising my hands up when I catch the scary ass glare on her face.

"Baby."

"Don't you dare laugh at me."

"I'm sorry," I tell her, quickly pulling her back when she tries to pull away. "Where are you going?"

"Away from you."

"The fuck you are."

She walks away from me anyway and I follow, picking her up by her waist to carry her up the beach.

"What the hell are you doing?!" she growls, thrashing and twisting in my arms, but I don't let her go.

Sugar We're Goin' Down by Fall Out Boy plays loudly from someone's car and I use it to my advantage, pushing her back against the wall behind the coffee shop where no one'll be able to hear her scream. She curses me to hell and back and I shut her up with my mouth, pinning her lower half with mine while I lift her thighs up around my waist. She smacks my chest and I let her do it, then she snatches my face and dips her head to bite my lips, hard and fucking painful.

My baby likes the fight.

She's embarrassed and upset and mad at me because I'm an idiot who doesn't know when to shut up, and if she wants to use me and my body to take her frustrations out, I'm not about to stop her.

It feels good when she scratches the sides of my neck, her teeth drawing the blood from my lips while she kisses me like she hates me. She rubs her pussy on my jeans and I squeeze her ass beneath my hoodie, reaching down between us with my free hand to feel how wet she is for me. She whimpers into my mouth and I pull her thong to the side, teasing her tongue with mine while I find her clit with my thumb.

"Oh my god, what is wrong with you?" she hisses, but she makes no move to stop me. "You're insane."

She's not wrong at this particular moment in time, but I don't tell her that. Instead I slide a finger inside her and fuck her with it, enjoying the way she moans and lifts her head to check no one's watching. I'm fully aware someone could walk around that corner and catch us like this, but I don't care. I need her *now* and she needs me just as much, even if she won't admit it.

I pop the button on my jeans and she lets out a shaky breath, her pretty blue eyes flashing with something that looks an awful lot like heat. "Jesus, Xan, we can't."

"Baby, how many times do I have to tell you?" I tease, pulling my dick out to rub her pussy with the tip. "We can do whatever the fuck we want, and if you think I won't fuck you right here against this wall in the middle of this stupid party to stake my claim, you're dead fucking wrong."

She drops her head back with a soft thud and I slip my way inside her, roughly digging my fingers into her ass while I fuck her hard and deep. I kiss her mouth and she yanks on my hair, suddenly back to mad, it seems.

"What is it, baby?" I ask, moving down to tease her neck with my teeth. "You hate me?"

She nods, the little liar.

"You're leaving me?"

She nods again and I bite her, not as hard as she bit me but hard enough to leave a little sting. She cries out and I smirk against the pulsing vein beneath my lips, slowing my pace a little bit while I kiss it better for her.

"Not a fucking chance," I whisper. "You can't just break up with me whenever you feel like it."

"Why the hell not?"

"Because you're mine and I'm yours. Because I love you and you love me. It's that fucking simple."

Her breath catches at my admission and I pull back an inch to look at her, raising a cocky ass brow when her pussy clenches around my dick.

"You like that?"

She nods and drops her forehead on mine, breathing heavily against my lips. "Say more stuff like that."

I laugh lightly and do as I'm told, mostly because I'm not done talking yet but also because I'll do any fucking thing she tells me to, no questions asked.

"I love you, Jordyn James," I tell her again, slower this time. "Whether you like it or not, *I love you* and I'm not letting you go. Not today. Not ever."

Her brows dip with worry and she opens her mouth to say something, but then she snaps it shut again and looks at something behind me. "What about–"

"Fuck them," I cut in, angrily banging the wall next to her head, but I'm not mad at her. "You think it matters what those stupid assholes say behind your back? You think it matters whether they think we're real or not?"

"I.." she trails off, blinking at me in surprise. "I don't.."

"It doesn't," I answer for her, looking her dead in the eye to ensure she hears me loud and clear. "All that matters is that *we* know."

She takes a breath and I kiss her again, sliding both hands down to her waist while I grind my hips against hers. She digs her nails into my shoulders and arches her back out for me, eagerly fucking me back hit for hit.

"I know you know, baby," I tell her, gently dragging her bottom lip out between my teeth. "I know you felt it then and I know you feel it now. I can't take my eyes off you. You're the only fucking girl I've ever seen."

"Oh, fuck," she moans, clinging to my neck while she becomes more and more desperate. "Harder, Xan."

Fuck, yes.

I give her what she wants and she comes almost instantly, her eyes rolling back in her head while she throbs and clenches around me. I groan into her mouth and drop my hands to her ass, crushing her between me and the wall while I mark her pussy with my own release. Her thighs shake and she locks her ankles behind my back, her chest moving in sync with mine while we both attempt to catch our breath.

"That was really stupid," she says after a while, her neck and cheeks flushed with heat while she looks around to check we're still alone.

"Fucking hot, though."

She smirks like the little devil she is and I smirk back, slowly running my hands over her body while I take her mouth with mine. I kiss her for I don't know how long, enjoying the way she lets me do it like she missed me just as much as I missed her today, then I set her down on her feet and sneak her around to the parking lot. We get to my car without being seen and I clean her up with a spare t-shirt, dropping to my knees in front of her to wipe my cum from the insides of her thighs.

"Did you eat yet?" I ask, looking up at her while I pull her thong back into place.

"No, but I've had about five iced coffees today."

I chuckle at that, standing up to toss my shirt back into the trunk. "You want me to go grab you some Chinese food?"

"Chinese food," she echoes, frowning while she looks off to the restaurant across the street. "Like, in a box?"

Little Devil

30

Jordyn

I lean back between Xan's legs and curl my toes in the sand beneath my feet, moaning to myself while I dangle my noodles into my mouth. "This is *so* good."

He laughs at me and I jab my elbow into his ribs, freezing mid chew when I spot Travis and Kian walking towards us with four beers and a lit joint of weed.

"Hey," Travis says, crouching down in front of me to tap my nose with his forefinger. "You still mad at me?"

"I wasn't mad at you, Trav," I admit, setting my food down on the ground to take the drink he passes me. "I was mad at your stupid cousin."

"That one right there, you mean?" Kian asks, smirking at us while he drops down on his ass next to me.

"Shut up."

He chuckles and I shake my head at him, smiling to myself while I look up at Xan over my shoulder. He's still flicking through the most recent photos on my camera, his eyes narrowed with a mixture of anger and jealousy. I took about seventy shots of the new friend I met today and he's shirtless in every single one of them, his body glistening with a light layer of sweat thanks to the mini football game I made him play for me.

"Fuckin' prick," he mutters at the last one, tightening his arm around my waist in a way that screams *mine*.

I laugh lightly and take the camera from him, discreetly hiding it between my back and his abs when I spot Penelope and Sienna walking by us on their way to the bar. Penelope rolls her eyes when she sees where I'm sitting and I work my jaw, snatching my chopsticks up while I prepare myself for the impending judgement.

I know Xan was right before, that I need to learn to stop worrying so much about the opinions of others and focus on what really matters, but that's a little hard for me to do considering the importance of image has been drilled into my brain since I was a child.

Sienna has the nerve to glare at me and Penelope stops walking, scrunching her nose while she tilts her head to get a better look at my wrist. "Oh my god, is that a *tattoo*?"

I raise a brow at that, casually eating my food while I wait for whatever she'll say next. Sienna knocks her elbow with hers and Penelope blinks, hitting me with a tight lipped smile that's as fake as my mother's chin.

"Pretty," she says, and I snort out a laugh, shaking my head at her when she grabs Sienna's forearm and drags her away from us.

Xan grins like he's proud of me and I bite my lip to hide mine, tipping my head back on his shoulder to run my free hand through his hair. "I love you."

"Sorry, what?"

"I love you," I repeat slowly, speaking through my teeth. "Asshole."

He smashes his mouth on mine and then moves down to my neck, kissing every inch of bare flesh he can find while I continue to eat the food he bought me.

"Ugh, you two are so fucking cute together, it hurts me," Kian complains, leaning over to steal the joint from Travis' mouth. "Why can't I have that?"

Travis turns his head to sneak a glance at him and I lift my camera, still chewing on my noodles while I snap a picture of them. They look up at me as one and I cock my head at my screen, zooming in a little bit and adjusting the shot to focus on their faces.

"You've already got it, you idiots," I say bluntly, sitting forward to pass it to them. "You're just too damn stubborn to admit it."

Little Devil

31

Xander

"I need to talk to you."

I laugh lightly at that, side eyeing Noah over my shoulder while I open my locker. "About what?"

"What the fuck do you think?" he bites out, quickly slapping his hand on the metal to slam it shut again.

His eyes flash with rage and I turn to face him fully, raising a cocky ass brow when he steps closer to me, his chest bumping mine, his nose an inch away.

"Careful, pretty boy," I taunt, refusing to back up like he was expecting me to. "You might be the king around here but I've got no fucking problem kicking your ass."

"She's *my* girl, you stupid freak," he hisses, ignoring everything I just said. "*Mine*."

I nod mockingly and open my mouth to tell him how wrong he is, but it seems he's not done acting like an entitled little bitch just yet.

"I had her first, and I'll have her last," he assures me, purposely moving his eyes over my form with a mixture of pity and disgust. "You're just a phase. One she'll get bored of real quick when she realizes how much of a fucking loser you are. And me? *I'm* the one she's gonna sleep next to every night for the rest of her life and there's nothing you can do to stop it."

"Is that right?" I draw out, amused by him and his lame ass attempt to get one up on me. "Did you just come up with that on the spot or did you practice in the mirror last night while I was balls deep inside *your* girl?"

His jaw ticks and I smirk, but then a sudden commotion behind me catches my attention and I turn my head, finding three uniformed police officers headed this way with my aunt Karen following closely behind them.

"Xander Reid?" one of them asks, motioning for me to step back out of the way. "Is this your locker?"

I frown and look between the three, but they're already opening it up with the combination I didn't give them yet. Students begin to hover around us and a few teachers come out from their classrooms to calm everyone down, but I'm still focused on the officers searching my locker, pulling my head back when they find several clear bags of cocaine and weed and pills and enough cash to get Jordyn through college.

"Oh, fuck," I whisper to myself, already knowing there's a real good chance I'm about to spend the next few years of my life in jail.

Karen's face burns with embarrassment and rage and I open my mouth to defend myself, but I don't get the chance to do that before one of the officers turns me around and cuffs my hands behind my back. He reads me my rights and Travis appears at my side, his eyes widening when he spots all the drugs behind me.

"*Mom*," he says, pleading her to do something, but she just shakes her head and lifts a hand to shut him up.

"They have a warrant, Travis. Be quiet and let them do their jobs."

He curses and I search the crowd for Jordyn, doing a double take at Noah when I find him talking to one of the teachers like the kiss ass he is. He shakes his head in mock disapproval and I bounce my eyes between his, laughing when it hits me because *fuck*, he *really* didn't want me to look inside that locker just now, did he?

"Piece of shit," I mutter, wincing when the officer behind me tightens the cuffs on my wrists. "Ow, you motherf– dude, that's not my kink."

He shoves me forward and I wiggle my hands to make myself more comfortable, looking up when I spot Jordyn walking around the corner just to freeze where she stands. Her face falls when she realizes what's happening and she tries to come towards me, but then Travis wraps his arm around her waist and holds her back, not letting go when she attempts to fight him off.

"*Xan*."

"Trav," I bite out. "Get your hands off my girl."

He does as he's told and she rushes me, her eyes filled with unshed tears while she pulls my face down to hers. "Don't say anything," she orders, quickly shoving her hand into my pocket to steal my keys. "Keep your mouth shut and wait for my lawyer to come get you."

I groan at that, dipping my head to catch her lips with mine. "You're too fucking good for me, Jordyn James."

A light laugh leaves her despite the circumstances and

she kisses me back, swallowing what looks like fear when they pull me away from her. The officer who cuffed me leads me out towards the parking lot and I look over my shoulder, ignoring the sea of eyes on me while I keep mine on Jordyn.

"That's my girlfriend," I say smugly, tilting my head at her to show him. "She's hot, right?"

He mutters something I don't catch and shoves my head down to throw me into the back of his car, angrily slamming the door in my face before he walks around to jump into the driver's seat. I blow out a breath and drop my head back on the head rest, frowning to myself when I realize how hungry I am.

"Can we stop and get some food on the way?"

32

Jordyn

The police car disappears out of the parking lot and I wipe my tears with my fingers, struggling not to choke on my heart considering it's lodged itself somewhere inside my throat. Students and teachers surround me on all sides and although their voices are loud and obnoxious, I do my best to drown them out and ignore the bad things they're saying about him.

Drug dealer.

Fucking freak.

Years..

I can't lose him like this.

Not for *years.*

I squeeze the car keys in my hand and force my feet to move, stopping mid step when the principal's voice rings out from somewhere behind me. "Miss James?"

"Yes?" I ask, turning around on the front steps to face

her fully.

She opens her mouth to say something but snaps it shut again, her eyes narrowing while she moves them over my school uniform. "Is your skirt rolled up?"

It is, but I'm not about to tell her that. "No."

"Can you prove it please?"

"I'd really rather not."

She raises a dark brow at that, crossing her arms over her chest with a look that resembles humor. That can't be right considering her nephew was just arrested for possession with intent, but it's still there all the same.

"I know what you're about to do and I'm warning you, I let you off once but I will not let it slide a second time."

"What's the punishment?"

"A three day suspension."

I nod and shrug my shoulders, struggling to care about anything but Xan in this particular moment. "I guess I'll be back on Friday, then."

With that, I turn around and walk away, taking my phone out from my purse on my way to Xan's Camaro. I find my mother's lawyer's number and hit the call button, but then I catch Penelope hiding behind a row of cars with her phone in her hand and a stupid little grin on her face, her bottom lip trapped between her teeth while she stares at the video playing on the small screen in front of her. The lawyer's voice fills my ear and I hang up without saying anything, not wanting Penelope to catch me spying on her. I can always call him back in a minute, but if she's watching what I think she's watching, I might not need him at all.

"It's not for me, you idiot," Noah hisses through the

phone. "This punk ass kid thinks he can steal my girlfriend and I want him gone. How much is it gonna take to get him put away for a few years, at least?"

I lock my jaw and step closer to her, quickly snatching the phone from her hand before she even realizes I'm here. She squeals and I shove her head back, turning my body away from her to watch the rest of it.

"Get me double that," he orders, pacing his bedroom with his shirt off and his phone pressed up to his ear. "Can you meet me now? I want it done by tomorrow."

After about ten seconds of him nodding and grabbing some clothes to pull on, the video cuts off and I glare at my former best friend, pulling the phone out of reach when she tries to snatch it from my hand.

"Did you take this without him knowing?"

She hesitates but nods, her eyes wide with panic. "I heard him talking when I went to his house last night and taped him before he saw me."

"Why?"

She squeezes her lips shut and I take a minute to think about my options, rewatching the whole thing so I know exactly what I'm dealing with here. As soon as I've come up with a plan that may or may not be very illegal and very stupid, I grab her forearm and drag her over to the passenger seat of Xan's car. She screams out in surprise but I ignore it, shoving her in to lock her inside. I'd never lay a hand on her under any other circumstances, but desperate times call for desperate measures. I can't risk leaving her here for her to rat me out to Noah the first chance she gets.

I jump in next to her and hit the gas, nervously flexing my small hands around the wheel while I drive us out of the parking lot.

"JJ, what the hell are you doing?"

Instead of answering her, I turn his music up in an attempt to calm my racing heart, willing myself to get through this without losing my nerve or throwing up.

You're too fucking good for me, Jordyn James.

But I can be bad when I want to be.

I can do this.

Ten minutes later, I pull up outside the police station and kill the ignition. "If you open your mouth or leave my side, I'll tell Noah what you did last night and make your life a living hell. Your choice, Pen."

She pulls her brows in but wisely follows me out of the car, her six inch stilettos tapping along the floor while she scurries to keep up with me. I push the main door open and Sheriff Brennan looks up from behind his desk, grinning when he sees it's me. He's Noah's mother's younger brother, a thirty seven year old man with dark blond hair and a killer pair of blue eyes. I used to have a minor crush on him when I was little, but then I realized he's just another narcissistic prick with his head up his brother in law's ass.

"Hey, sweetheart–"

"I need to talk to you about Xander Reid," I cut in, walking over to stand directly in front of him.

His mouth pops open and he starts to say something, but then the door I know leads to the jail cells swings open and crashes against the wall with a loud bang, making everyone jump.

"Cocky little shit," the officer who took Xan spits out, angrily ripping his hands through his hair while he moves for the coffee machine in the corner.

I hide a knowing grin and the sheriff rolls his eyes, leaning back in his seat with his arms crossed over his wide chest, his attention on me. "You were saying?"

"He didn't do it," I tell him, keeping my voice low to ensure no one else hears me. "Noah bought the drugs last night and set it all up for Xander to take the fall."

He sighs at that, shaking his head at me the way he used to when I was ten. "Look, JJ, I don't know what's going on between you and this new kid but you're being ridiculous. My nephew would never–"

I raise a brow and press play on the video in my hand, turning the volume down a bit before I turn it around to show him the screen. Noah's one sided conversation shocks him into silence and he narrows his eyes, his nostrils flaring while he watches it to the end.

"Have you lost your mind?" he whispers, leaning over the desk between us with his hands clenched into fists. "Taping someone without consent is illegal, something *you* could go to jail for. Did you really think you'd be able to show this in court?"

"We're not going to court," I inform him, casually twisting the phone around in my hand. "If you don't release him and drop the charges *today*, I'll send this to everyone I know. Every student at Lakewood, every teacher, every parent, every neighbor.. *everyone.*"

"JJ.." he warns, speaking through his teeth. "I love you like a niece, you know that. But blackmailing the *sheriff* is just about the dumbest thing you've ever done."

I nod because he's right about that, but I also know how this family works. Much like my mother, they treasure their image like diamonds. They thrive on power and respect and loyalty, and if this town were to find out that their future mayor has a tendency to frame innocent people for shit they didn't do, I'm sure that would reflect very, very badly on them.

The threat hangs in the air between us and he sighs, angrily shoving the papers on his desk before barking his orders at the officer by the coffee machine. "Release the kid and get the mayor up here."

Penelope's jaw drops and I smirk, keeping hold of the evidence while I walk her outside. "You can go now."

"But.." she trails off, looking between me and the building in confusion. "What about Noah?"

"I don't give a fuck about Noah."

"Okay, then," she mouths, awkwardly clearing her throat before speaking again. "What about my phone?"

"I'm sure you can afford a new one," I mutter, side eyeing her when she makes no move to leave. "What?"

"I, uh.. you asked me why I did it and I just.."

"Spit it out, Pen."

"I only wanted to lay a little harmless blackmail on him to make him mine," she admits, shrugging with a look that seems an awful lot like sadness. "I never would have showed it to anyone if you hadn't heard it before."

I frown at that, unsure why she'd need to blackmail him when she's already fucking him on a regular basis.

"He doesn't want more with me, JJ," she says quietly, somehow reading my mind. "He only wants you."

I stare at her face and she walks away, stopping in the middle of the parking lot when I call out to her.

"Penelope."

She sighs heavily and turns around to face me, silently

waiting for whatever I'm about to say.

"You deserve better."

She nods slowly and moves to leave, not so discreetly wiping the tears from her cheeks before she disappears out of sight. I chew the inside of my cheek and look back at the main door, nervously pacing back and forth while I wait for Xan to come out.

"You look tired, sweetie," Kian tells me, dropping down on the front steps beside me to wrap his arm around my shoulders. "You want us to go grab you one of those iced coffees you like from that shop on the beach?"

I nod and smile at him, gently scratching the spot beneath Bear's ears in an attempt to comfort him. School ended just over an hour ago and I asked him and Travis to go check on him, knowing he'd been on his own all day while I've been waiting for Xan to get out of jail. They said he was restless and upset and *scaring the shit out of them*, as they put it, so I told them to put him in the car and bring him to me.

The boys drive away without me and I look at the door again, honest to god contemplating storming in there and giving those assholes a piece of my mind. A few more minutes pass and I almost do it, but then Bear lifts his head and whines at something in front of us, standing up to pull on the heavy leash in my hand. I look that way and find a black limo pulled up outside the station, quickly slapping a hand over my mouth when I realize Alec Reid and Isla Montgomery are climbing out through the back door. He's dressed in black jeans and a t-shirt and she's dressed in leggings and a loose tank top, both wearing matching ball caps to hide their identities, I'm assuming.

"Oh, shit," I whisper to myself, nervous as hell and completely unprepared. "Bear, wait–"

But he doesn't stop pulling me down towards them.

"..still don't understand why I have to be here," Xan's mother mutters, adjusting the hat on her head while she falls in line beside her husband.

"Because you're his mom."

"He's *eighteen*, Alec," she argues, rolling her eyes when she catches the disappointed glare on his face. "We all agreed he'd be Karen's problem from now on. Why couldn't she handle this by herself?"

"Will you get a fucking grip?" he bites out, snatching her upper arm to pull her chest to his. "She already told us she's got no choice but to expel him after what he did today. He's not her responsibility anymore, Isla."

Her jaw ticks and she slaps his hand from her arm, looking up at him without an ounce of fear there. "I don't want him back at home."

"Yeah, well, that's good, because he's going to jail," he deadpans, doing a quick double take when he catches the big ass dog pawing at his shin. "Bear."

Xan's parents look up at me and I clear my throat, struggling to think of anything but the very private conversation I just overheard.

"Um.. hi," I say lamely, offering a small wave because I don't know what to do with my hands. "Mr Reid, Mrs Montgomery. I'm JJ James, Xander's girlfriend."

Their dark brows jump as one and I die a little on the inside, cursing myself when I catch the clear look of surprise on their faces.

"I'm sorry, did he not–"

"He told us about you," his mom assures me, pausing a second to move her light hazel eyes over my form. "We just didn't expect you to be so.."

"You look like a really nice girl," her husband finishes for her, half smiling to himself while he reaches down to scratch Bear's head.

"Thank you, sir."

He smiles for real this time and removes his hat from his head, scrubbing a hand through his dark hair the same way Xan does. "Have they told you anything yet?"

"Yeah, they said they'd release him but that was hours ago," I explain. "I was just about to–"

"Wait, why is he being released?" his mother asks, frowning while she looks up at the building behind me.

"Because it wasn't him."

"Of course it wasn't," she says dryly, sighing heavily when she catches the look I must be giving her. "Listen, honey, I don't know what he told you about the drugs but I can assure you he's lying. This is just what he does."

I laugh lightly at that, shaking my head in disgust while I step back to look between the two. I was willing to drop what I heard just now because it's been a long fucking day for all of us and I'm sure they're tired after getting up at the crack of dawn to catch a five hour flight from LA, but I won't stand here and allow them to talk shit about Xan to my face.

"You know what? How about *you* listen while I assure *you* something?" I bite out, speaking slowly to ensure they hear me loud and clear. "Your son is a good person. He might not be perfect but he's loyal and honest and sweet and funny and I *know* his brother would be proud of him. You should count yourselves lucky to call him yours, because I sure as hell do."

They stare at me in shock and I pass the leash to Xan's dad, ignoring my guilt for yelling at my boyfriend's parents because *fuck them*, they deserved it.

"Where are you going?" Alec calls, unable to follow me considering Bear's not allowed inside the station.

"To find out what's taking so damn long," I call back, leaving them outside while I push my way through the main door.

33

Xander

"Reid," the moody officer barks, opening the cell door to let me out. "Let's go."

Fucking finally.

I force myself up to stand and stretch my arms above my head, tired as shit after spending I don't know how long locked up in here by myself.

"You don't get many criminals in this town, huh?" I guess, sighing dramatically when he continues to ignore me and my questions. "Hey, will you make a quick run to Starbucks for m–"

He shoves me forward and I stumble, chuckling to myself when I catch the tick in his jaw. At first I assume he's taking me to the interview room, but then he leads me out the way we came in earlier and I frown at him, quickly facing forward again when I hear the sound of her voice by the sheriff's desk.

"..your hands off me," she growls, angrily kicking her

legs out while they cuff her wrists behind her back. "I am Jordyn fucking James and I will have your jobs–"

"Baby," I laugh, and she stops fighting them, instantly relaxing when she sees me standing here.

"Hey," the guy beside me hisses, speaking to the two officers restraining her. "That's the sheriff's niece and the mayor's future daughter in law, you idiots. Take those off her before they come back. *Now.*"

They do as they're told and she huffs out an aggravated breath, ignoring the *daughter in law* comment while she walks over to me. She wraps her arms around my neck and I pick her up, gently lifting her thighs up around my waist to hold her close.

"Baby, what did you do?" I ask quietly, still amused by her little outburst just now.

"I fixed it," she tells me, grinning like a bad bitch while she lowers her mouth to mine.

I kiss her back and squeeze her thighs with both hands, laughing lightly when the officer who walked me out just now looks like he wants to hit me for it.

"I told you she was mine," I say smugly, setting her down on her feet to follow him to the front desk.

He shakes his head in annoyance and tosses me my stuff, gesturing for me to sign out before he waves me off with a half assed flick of his wrist. "Go away."

Okay, then.

Jordyn takes my hand and I follow her outside, confused as to why they're letting me go so soon, but I'm not about to argue. I find my cigarettes and take one out with my free hand, side eyeing her while I lift my lighter to burn the tip. She opens her mouth like she's about to explain it to me, but then my dog appears at my feet and I look down at him in surprise, not missing the way Jordyn cringes and drops her eyes like she's embarrassed about something. I pull my brows in and scratch Bear's head, looking up to find both of my parents standing behind him.

"Hey.." I say slowly, glancing between them and Jordyn before I settle on them. "It wasn't me."

My mom nods to herself and my dad looks like he's hiding a grin, leaning over to pass me the leash he's holding. "We know, kid," he tells me, tilting his head at Jordyn, his eyes filled with adoration and pride. "That's quite a girl you've got there."

I grin back and wrap my arm around her waist, pulling her into me to kiss her forehead. "You're just full of surprises today, aren't you, princess?"

She laughs lightly and hides her face in my chest, jumping against me when a familiar voice rings out from somewhere beside us. "JJ!"

Oh, fuck.

"Oh, fuck," she whispers to herself, looking over to find her mother at the bottom of the steps with a glare on her face and her hands propped on her hips.

She's standing next to Noah fucking Campbell and an older looking man I assume is the mayor, all three looking mad as hell with their eyes on us.

"What on earth do you think you're doing?" her mom asks, staring at Jordyn with a look that promises pain and suffering and all that bad shit.

"Mom," Jordyn hisses, pleading her with her eyes not to make a scene. "Can we not do this her–"

"No, you stupid girl, we're doing this now," she cuts in,

her face red with unfiltered fury. "Your future is at stake here and we will not allow you to throw it away for this delinquent *boy*," she sneers, glaring at the cigarette in my hand before she moves her attention back to her daughter. "If you don't come home with us right this second I will kick you out of my house and you will have *nothing* left. I mean it, JJ. It's either him or us. Make your choice."

"For fuck's sake, Elizabeth, there is no *choice*," Noah bites out, stepping closer like he's about to snatch Jordyn's arm, but then Bear growls and yanks on the leash in my hand to go for him, making him jump.

"Jesus Christ," he mutters, damn near shitting himself while he falls back in line beside his father.

Bear continues to bark at him from his spot in front of Jordyn and she looks at me, leaning up on her tiptoes to speak over my lips. "Do you dare me?"

I shake my head at that, tightening my arm around her waist until her hips bump mine. "Not this time, baby. If you're doing this, do it because you want to. Do it because you want *me*."

"I do want you," she says without hesitation. "It's always gonna be you, new boy."

I smirk and she smirks back, looking over when she spots Travis and Kian standing with my parents behind us. I didn't even hear them show up, but they don't seem bothered by the drama unfolding around us. Trav bumps my fist and Kian grins, leaning over to pass Jordyn the iced coffee he must have bought for her.

"Thank you, gorgeous," she says sweetly, lifting the straw to her mouth to take a sip.

Her mother mutters something I don't catch and folds her arms over her chest, her nostrils flaring while she bounces her eyes between me and Jordyn. "He's gonna ruin your life," she tells her, but it's not a plea for her to stay.

She says it like a fact.

One last *fuck you* to the daughter she can't control anymore.

Jordyn shrugs and looks at the mayor, shaking her ass while she walks over to pass him the phone in her hand. He glares down at her and she tosses me my keys, sliding her fingers through mine while she pulls me back towards my car in the parking lot.

"How bad were you today, princess?"

"Bad enough to ditch school, get myself suspended, kidnap Penelope *and* blackmail the sheriff," she says proudly, ticking them off on her fingers. "I also yelled at your parents and threatened the police with a lot of curse words. I even said *motherfucker* once."

"For real?"

"For real," she echoes, and I drag my lip out between my teeth, shamelessly moving my eyes over her body in that sexy little uniform I love so much.

"Hey, pretty boy?" I call out, hitting him with a smug ass grin while I flip him off over my shoulder. "Fuck you."

His jaw ticks with rage and Jordyn laughs, quickly lowering my hand to my side while she opens the back door for Bear. The three of us jump inside and I start the ignition, casually smoking the last of my cigarette while Jordyn pulls her seatbelt on over her chest.

"Xan, don't–"

I hit the gas and her mother squeals, stepping back with her mouth hanging open and her hands covering her heart. Jordyn shakes her head at me and I toss my roach out the window, keeping one eye on the road while I lean over to tilt her chin up with my free hand.

"I love you, baby girl."

She smiles at that, real and honest and *happy*. "That's good, because you're stuck with me now."

34

Jordyn

"Xan," I complain, leaning back against his headboard, my hands fisting the sheet either side of me.

"What, baby?"

"Can you be serious for a second?" I rasp out, but I still find myself rolling my hips up to grind my clit on his tongue. "I don't have any clothes here."

"You can wear mine."

"I don't have a job."

"You can be my live in stripper," he offers, slowly moving his hands down to squeeze the backs of my thighs. "I'll tip you *real* good for this ass."

"I don't even have a toothbrush."

"I'll take you out after and buy you one."

I feign annoyance and prop myself up on my elbows, rolling my eyes when I catch the amusement on his face. "Do you have to have an answer for everything?"

He laughs at me and pushes me back down, dipping his head to flick his tongue over my clit. My hips buck and my problems fall away from me, my eyes rolling back at the way he attacks my pussy with his mouth. He slides a finger inside me and I reach down to run my nails through his hair, frowning when he snatches my hands with one of his and pins them to my stomach.

"Don't come yet," he orders, and I whine like a needy little brat, barely managing to keep myself on the edge without falling off.

"Why not?"

Instead of answering me, he moves back a bit and pulls out a small plastic bag from I don't know where, smirking at me when he catches the confusion on my face. It's a new tongue bar – a pink and purple one with a silver ball at the bottom and a few silicone spikes on the top part. He switches them out with ease and I watch him do it, dropping my jaw when a faint buzzing sound fills my ears.

"What the hell is tha–"

"Shut up and take it," he cuts in, roughly snatching my waist to yank me down to him.

My eyes widen with a mixture of shock and heat and he lies down between my legs, kissing his way from my navel to my hip bone with a slowness that drives me crazy.

"Oh, fuck," I moan, somehow knowing what's about to happen before it comes. "Xan, please–"

He flicks my clit with his tongue and I scream, curling in on myself to grab onto his hair with my hand. He laughs lightly and I pull the strands at the top, tipping my head back on my shoulders at the feel of it. It's fucking *vibrating*, teasing me and setting me on fire from the inside out. He tilts his head to get the angle I like and I whimper, shamelessly rubbing my pussy on his mouth to chase the high I'm craving.

"Xan, make me come."

He fucks me with his fingers and I fall apart, shaking and writhing beneath him while he continues to lick my clit with his new toy. My heart races in my ears and I fall back against the pillows, quickly pulling him up to wrap my arms around his neck.

"Where did you get that?"

"I ordered it online last night when I was looking for you in the city," he explains, opening his mouth to turn it off with his thumb and forefinger. "I figured if you kept hiding from me I could steal you away at school today and force you to talk to me with my tongue."

I grin like an idiot and he kisses my lips, leaning up on one elbow beside my head while he strokes my outer thigh with his free hand. I wrap my legs around his waist and run my hands over his shoulders, secretly loving the way he feeds me my own release.

"Baby," he says, nudging my head to the side to move his mouth down to my neck.

"Yeah?"

"I'm gonna put my dick in your ass."

I moan at that, scraping my nails over his scalp to keep him there. "You're so sweet to me."

He chuckles and reaches out to grab the lube from the nightstand, blindly flicking the cap off the top to cover his fingers with it. He reaches down between us and I spread my legs out for him, breathing hard against the side of his face while he circles my hole with the middle one. We've done this part before but we've never gone any further than two fingers, and I can't figure out whether I should be excited or terrified.

"Don't be scared, baby," he whispers, taunting me with his words and his tongue while he licks the throbbing vein in my neck. "I'm gonna make you come so fucking hard."

I whimper and he sinks his teeth into my flesh, marking me with yet another hickey I'll have to cover up with concealer later. He kisses me there and stretches me out for what feels like hours, then he finally puts me out of my misery and pulls his fingers out, fisting his cock to cover it with lube before teasing my ass with it.

"Tell me if it hurts too bad, okay?"

I nod and he slides the tip in, watching me closely for my reaction while my body gets used to the burn. He only fucks me about half way at first, clearly not wanting to push me by going too fast too soon, but then I lift my hips up and he curses, his dark hair falling over his eyes while he presses our foreheads together.

"You wanna take it all?"

I nod again and he gives it to me, rocking his hips out a little more until he's buried all the way inside me. I cry out and he nips my bottom lip, his eyes darkening with heat when he catches the look in mine.

"Xan," I plead, unsure what I'm even begging for, but he doesn't seem to mind.

"Open your mouth and stick your tongue out."

I do as I'm told and he sucks on it, groaning against me while he rubs my clit with his thumb.

Oh, shit, that feels good.

My legs start to shake and I rake my fingers through his hair, desperately clinging to him while he fucks me hard and deep. The stretch still hurts a little bit, but the way he's working my clit like that makes up for it and then some. He does something with his fingers and I come loudly – *too* loudly – quickly slapping a hand over my mouth to cover the sound. He smirks and shakes his head at me, snatching my wrists to pin them down to the pillows above me. He grinds on me and I squeeze his hips with my thighs, throwing my head back while he sets me off beyond control.

"Fuck, baby," he chokes out, his hard body locked up against mine while he fills my ass with his cum. "*Fuck.*"

I shiver and he links our fingers together, kissing his way from my throat to my collarbone. A few minutes go by and he pulls out slowly, careful not to rip me apart with the piercing on the tip of his cock. He cleans us both up with a towel and I sit up to throw one of his shirts over my head, nervously chewing my lip while my worries come rushing back to me.

"Xan–"

"Sweetie, your mom's coming," Kian says from the pool house door, stopping to smirk at me when he spots the bottle of lube on the bed. "Oh, you naughty girl."

"I.. wait, *what?*"

Her distant voice fills my ears and I curse, quickly grabbing some leggings to pull them up over my hips. Xan finds a pair of sweats to wear but leaves his shirt off, following closely behind me while we head outside with Travis and Kian. Bear walks over to stand in front of me and I scratch his head, looking up to find my mother talking quietly with Xan's parents and the principal by the pool.

"Mom," I call, effectively stealing her attention away

from them. "What are you doing here?"

"I need to talk to you."

"About what?"

"College," she answers, curling her lip while she bounces her eyes between me and Xan. "I don't agree with your choice and I never will, but I'm willing to pay for you to go to school in Seattle next fall."

My heart skips a beat and I pull my brows in, confused considering she was dead set on disowning me a couple of hours ago. "Why?"

"Why do you think?" she asks, gritting her teeth like it's physically painful for her to get the words out. "If I let you run off with no money and no purpose in life, people will talk and spread rumors about me. I won't let you ruin my reputation more than you already have, and having a daughter who has to *work* for a living is even more embarrassing than one who abandons her responsibilities to become an artist."

"Photographer."

"Yes, that," she says distractedly, waving a hand while she pulls her phone out from her purse. "I'll have the girls set up an interview once you receive your acceptance letter and we'll make it look like a positive thing, tell them you're down to earth or something along those lines. I'm sure we can find a way to twist it to make me look like a caring, supportive mother."

"I'm sure," I mutter, refraining from calling her out on her selfishness because it's pointless.

She's not about to change who she is or what she believes in – not today, at least – and I honestly have no desire to force her to do so. I can't make her love me just because, and even though it still hurts a little bit, I'm not about to try and force that, either.

"You can keep your trust fund and your car, but I still expect you to do exceedingly well at school and keep and eye on your.. *image*," she stresses, thankfully not stupid enough to say *weight* in front of all these people. "No more skipping classes, no more suspensions, and no more ridiculous tattoos. Do I make myself clear?"

I raise a brow at that, crossing my arms over my chest with my head cocked to the side. "Yes, Mother."

"Good," she says, putting her phone away before smoothing her hands over the front of her dress. "I assume you're not coming home with me?"

I shake my head and she sighs out an angry breath, but she doesn't own me anymore and it seems she knows it.

Xan wraps his arms around me from behind and she hits him with a look of disgust, not even bothering to acknowledge anyone else before she turns around and walks back to the car waiting on the driveway. Silence follows and Xan's mother frowns, looking from her to us and then back to her again.

"What a bitch."

"*Isla*," her sister scolds, but the rest of us are all laughing, Xan's dad included.

He dips his head to hide it and shoves his hands into his pockets, clearing his throat before he looks between me and his son. "Are you kids hungry yet? We were just about to order some food before we go."

"Wait, you're leaving tonight?" Xan asks, looking a little disappointed when they both nod. "Why?"

"I've got work at five tomorrow morning and your mother's got an appointment with her therapist."

"Thank you, Alec," Isla says dryly. "I'm sure everybody here needed to know that."

"Honey, most of them already know what a raging lunatic you are," he throws back, smirking right at her when he catches the look on her face. "It's nothing to be embarrassed about."

"You are such a prick."

"That's not what you said in the car just now," he mutters, earning himself a nasty glare and a hard slap to the chest. "You hit like a girl."

"I swear to god, I could kill you."

"Try it."

"Don't tempt me."

I pinch my lips together and look up at Xan, pulling my brows in when I find him grinning like a dumbass.

"What are you so happy about?"

"They're arguing," he whispers, side eyeing his parents while he dips his head to kiss the crook of my neck.

"And that's a good thing?"

"Baby, that's an *awesome* thing," he tells me, tightening his arms around my waist while he moves to speak in my ear. "I dare you to take a shower with me."

"Right now?" I hiss, my cheeks heating when he nods and pulls me back towards the pool house. "What about dinner with your parents?"

"It'll take at least a half hour for the food to get here," he points out, nipping my earlobe. "I'll make you come hard and fast, I promise."

My pussy throbs at that, and I almost moan.

"Goddamnit, Xan."

Travis and Kian both laugh at us and Xan wiggles his eyebrows, but then he stops walking and looks at our principal over my head. "Am I expelled?"

"No, you're not expelled," she assures him, lifting a hand when he starts to say something else. "And yes, JJ can move in with you for the rest of senior year. You've both been sleeping here every night anyway, so it's really no different than before, is it?"

I fail to hide my amusement and she winks at me, playfully shaking her head at us when Xan picks me up and throws me over his shoulder. I let out a squeal and he squeezes my ass over my leggings, chuckling to himself while he carries me through to the bathroom in the pool house. He turns the water on and sets me down on my feet, quickly ripping his shirt over my head before he's back on me again, squeezing my sides and owning my body in a way that makes me crazy. He kisses me and I melt against him, lifting my hands to run my fingers through his messy purple hair.

"We're going to Washington, baby girl," he rasps, grabbing my waistband to push it down over my ass. "Are you happy?"

"Xan, I'm so fucking happy, I could cry."

He grins and quickly sheds the rest of our clothes, backing me up into the shower to push me up against the wall beneath the water. He pulls my head back by my hair and kisses me again, blindly reaching over to grab the shower gel from the side. I run my hands over his abs and he washes his dick with his free hand, groaning when I reach down to help him do it.

"Hey, Jordyn?" he asks, breathing hard against my lips.

"What, Xan?"

Little Devil

He pulls back a bit to look at me and smirks like a bad boy, his nose brushing mine while he teases my ribs with his fingertips. "I dare you to love me forever."

EPILOGUE

seven years later

Xander

"I hate this, Xan," she chokes out, dropping her head to rest it on her forearms. "I hate *you*."

I hide a grin and lean over to hold her hair for her, gently rubbing circles on her back to help ease her through it. She tells me that every time I get her pregnant, but then the morning sickness goes away and she goes right back to loving me.

Most of the time.

She finally stops throwing up and stands up to walk over to the bathroom sink, glaring at me through the mirror while she snatches her toothbrush and brushes her teeth. This is the third time she's been pregnant in four years, and I'm pretty sure the only thing she's thinking about right now is how much jail time she'd get for killing me in my sleep.

"Baby–"

"Don't talk to me."

Little Devil

I snap my mouth shut and roll my lips in, silently staring at her ass while she bends over to wash her face. She looks so fucking sexy today, her tight little body wrapped up in a short floral sundress with her tanned legs on full display. As soon as she turns around, she catches me looking and tosses her hand towel on the counter, clipping the back of my head while she passes me on her way out. I laugh quietly and move to follow her, not missing the way she smirks at me over her shoulder while she walks away from me.

There she is.

She shakes her ass on purpose and I smack it, quickly stealing a kiss from her lips before I stalk her all the way down to the back yard. It's her twenty fifth birthday today and most of our friends and family are here to spend the day with her, except her mother because of course the evil queen couldn't take a day out of her busy schedule for her own flesh and blood. She married some rich asshole named Pierre a couple years ago and they spend most of their time in Europe with his children. It still pisses me off that Elizabeth doesn't appreciate her daughter for who she is and what she's made for herself, but Jordyn's more than used to it by now and doesn't let it bother her as much as she used to. She's too busy with me and the boys and her big ass studio to give two shits about her absent mother. As soon as she graduated college four years ago, she became a full time photographer and now she's got a waiting list three times the size of mine. She's worked for celebrities and authors and even shot a few album covers for Justin and a handful of other artists she's met through him over the years.

She's fucking amazing and beautiful and *mine*, and I honestly don't know how I managed to convince her to spend the rest of her life with me.

The humid air hits us as soon as we walk outside and Jordyn grins, winking at me before she makes her way over to the barbecue set up by the hot tub. She freaked out over the cold every winter when we lived in Seattle so we moved to LA the day after her last exam, bought ourselves this big ass house with a huge pool and more bedrooms than we know what to do with. I suggested we fill them up with kids and my parents were fully on board with that idea, but Jordyn just laughed at me and told me to go fuck myself.

"Dude, your wife is so fucking hot," Justin informs me, snatching a beer from the cooler to uncap it with his teeth. "Maybe I should get me one of those."

"A wife?"

"A pregnant girl," he jokes, still staring at her chest while he lifts his drink up to his mouth.

I snort and shove his head away, secretly hoping it makes him choke on his own tongue. Jordyn's jaw hit the floor when she met him for the first time and I almost broke his nose, but it's been seven years and he hasn't tried to fuck her yet, so I consider that a win.

Our friend Monica shows up a little while later and hits us both with a fake smile that screams *fuck you, losers*, then she hugs my wife and moves on to say hi to my parents and the kids. She's one of the best tattoo artists I've ever met and she works her ass off seven days a week, which is why she's pretending to be pissed at me for closing the shop today and forcing her to take a day off. She loves Jordyn like a sister, though, and she still shows up for her birthday every year without fail.

Justin stares at my employee and bites the edge of his fist, groaning into it when she pulls her shirt off and drops her jeans, revealing a black bikini underneath and a body covered in ink. She's told him she's into girls about a hundred times by this point but he doesn't let that stop him, the fucker.

Little Devil

"Goddamn, that ass," he hisses loudly, clearly trying to get a rise out of her. "Mon, will you let me lick your pussy if I cover your eyes firs–"

"Hey," Jordyn cuts him off, looking up at him with a brow raised and a sharp knife in her hand. "Watch your mouth by my kids."

"Sorry."

She shakes her head at him and I laugh, walking over to see what she's chopping considering me and the boys already cooked everything we had earlier. She drops down in her seat at the table and starts making herself a chicken and bacon burger, then she grabs a pineapple ring and places it right there in the middle. I scrunch my nose in disgust and she grins, lifting it up to her mouth to take a big ass bite out of it.

"No, baby, you can't–"

"Can't *what?*" she asks, speaking around her food. "I'm pregnant *and* I'm the birthday girl. Fight me."

I hide my amusement and lean back against the table to watch her eat it, looking up when Nikolas comes rushing over to me from across the yard. Bear follows behind him like he always does and I scoop him up in my arms, running a hand through his dark hair until it sticks out like mine does. He's three years old and he can talk until he runs out of oxygen, but I still can't understand a damn word that comes out of his mouth.

He tries to say something to me and I frown, looking at Jordyn for help.

"He wants to go in the pool."

"How do you know that?"

"Because he just told you," she draws out, leaning over

to wipe her hands with a napkin.

I frown some more but give my son what he wants, quickly shoving his life jacket on before stealing Jameson from my mom to take him with us. She feigns a pout at the loss of her grandson and crosses her arms over her chest, making us all laugh. My dad pokes her ribs and she smacks his hand away, but I don't miss the sideways look she gives him that makes me want to gag. They gradually started working things out after they kicked me out in high school and now they're pretty much back to the way they were before my brother was killed – disgusting as fuck, if you ask me – and even though I'm sure they still hate me for it sometimes, they never hesitate to tell me how much they love me and how proud they are of me and my girl.

Jameson squeals when he realizes where we're going and smiles up at me, wrapping his tiny little arms around my neck while I lower him and his big brother into the pool. He's eighteen months old and he's the chillest kid I've ever met. Where Nikolas can run around for hours without stopping, Jameson would rather sit on my lap and stare at a book all day long.

He's fucking perfect.

They both are.

"Go, daddy, go," Nik laughs, thrashing his arms and kicking his legs out beneath the surface.

"Let go," Jordyn explains, laughing to herself while she leans over to grab her camera from the table.

I let him go and he swims off as fast as he can, his life jacket holding him up while he spins around and splashes himself with water. I mess around with the boys for a while and then Travis and Kian jump in to steal them away from me, both them and Justin arguing over who their favorite uncle is.

It's Kian, hands down, but I don't encourage the little brat by telling him that.

I'm just about to get out and grab us all another drink each, but then Jordyn takes her dress off and lifts her arms up to tie her hair in a messy bun, looking hot as fucking sin dressed in a white bikini with a strapless top and two sets of strings hanging from her hips. She sits down on the edge of the pool and I move to stand between her legs, slowly sliding my arms around her waist to kiss her stomach. We're having a girl this time, just like I always wanted, and I swear to god I almost choked when she asked me if we could call her Frankie.

I kiss her again and she reaches out to run a hand through my hair, watching me closely while she slides her tongue bar over her teeth. She finally let me have my way with her on her nineteenth birthday, and even though she cursed me to hell and back because it hurt like a bitch, I know she loves being able to drive me bat shit crazy the same way I do her. And when she lies on her back with her head off the edge of the bed and lets me fuck her mouth while I'm eating her pussy..

God fucking damn it.

"You wanna pretend you're sick so everyone has to fuck off home?" I whisper, lifting her up to pull her into the water with me. "I'll get my parents to take the kids and we can spend the rest of the day in bed."

"You're awful," she whispers back, almost annoyed, but I don't miss the tease in her tone.

"You'll still love me forever, though, right?"

"Yes," she answers, sighing heavily against my lips. "It's very inconvenient, you know? Loving you."

I smirk at that, carefully pulling her thighs up around my waist to ensure I don't squish my daughter between us.

My dick rests against her clit through our swimsuits and she digs her nails into my neck, quickly looking over to ensure our boys aren't watching, then she dips her head and smashes her mouth on mine, making me laugh.

Inconvenient, my ass.

The End.

Acknowledgements

To my husband and son, and our beautiful friends and family: thank you for putting up with me. I know I'm an antisocial basket case who refuses to leave my writing cave, but I appreciate you all for sticking by me and supporting me anyway.

To Samantha La Mar: thank you *so* much for everything you've done for me and this book over the last few months. I mean.. just LOOK AT IT! *cue swoony heart eyes and fire emojis* I love you and your massive heart, and I'm so freaking lucky to have you in my life.

To my favourite book besties, Geissa (AKA Cece Perez), Pamela, Chrissy, Lisa, Rachael and Jocelyn, and every single author, reader, reviewer and bookstagrammer I've come to know since I started this journey a year ago: thank you all from the bottom of my heart. I couldn't cope in this terrifying industry without you.

To my incredible beta readers, ARC team and the reviewers at TalkNerdy2Me: thank you so much for your early feedback on this book. You never fail to encourage me and big me up when I'm shitting myself and I love you for that.

To Lacy Dyson: thank you for pineapple chicken burgers. I tried one like you told me to. It was.. horrifying, to be honest. But Jordyn likes them so you can consider that a win.

Last but not least, thank you to every single one of you for picking up this book and reading it. I am eternally grateful.

All my love,

Bethany ♥

Also by Bethany Winters

The Kingston Brothers Series

Kings of Westbrook High

Reckless at Westbrook High

Coming Soon

Romance After Dark: A Taboo Anthology

Dirty Love

About the Author

Bethany lives in South Wales with her husband and their four year old son. Her favourite things are books, tea, pizza, popcorn and Machine Gun Kelly, although her husband is still pretty mad about that last one. When she's not writing, she's either reading or daydreaming about the books she's read, or raiding Amazon for pretty paperbacks to hoard.

Join Bethany Winters' Reader Group for the latest teasers, giveaways and all that fun stuff.

Sign up for her newsletter to receive (irregular) updates on what she's reading and writing about, new releases, bonus scenes and more.

https://bethanywinters.co.uk/subscribe

Find Bethany on:

Facebook | Instagram | Goodreads

Amazon | Pinterest

Made in United States
Troutdale, OR
12/28/2023

16495560R00166